A Note to P[arents]

DK READERS is a compelling pro[gram] for beginning readers, designed in conjunction with leading literacy experts, including Dr. Linda Gambrell, Professor of Education at Clemson University. Dr. Gambrell has served as President of the National Reading Conference and the College Reading Association, and has recently been elected to serve as President of the International Reading Association.

Beautiful illustrations and superb full-color photographs combine with engaging, easy-to-read stories to offer a fresh approach to each subject in the series. Each DK READER is guaranteed to capture a child's interest while developing his or her reading skills, general knowledge, and love of reading.

The five levels of DK READERS are aimed at different reading abilities, enabling you to choose the books that are exactly right for your child:

Pre-level 1: Learning to read
Level 1: Beginning to read
Level 2: Beginning to read alone
Level 3: Reading alone
Level 4: Proficient readers

The "normal" age at which a child begins to read can be anywhere from three to eight years old. Adult participation through the lower levels is very helpful for providing encouragement, discussing storylines, and sounding out unfamiliar words.

No matter which level you select, you can be sure that you are helping your child learn to read, then read to learn!

LONDON, NEW YORK, MELBOURNE,
MUNICH, AND DELHI

For Dorling Kindersley
Designer Sandra Perry
Senior Editor Laura Gilbert
Design Manager Rob Perry
Managing Editor Catherine Saunders
Art Director Lisa Lanzarini
Publishing Manager Simon Beecroft
Category Publisher Alex Allan
Production Editor Sean Daly
Production Controller Nick Seston

Reading Consultant
Linda B. Gambrell, Ph.D.

First published in the United States in 2010
by DK Publishing
375 Hudson Street,
New York, New York 10014

10 11 12 13 14 10 9 8 7 6 5 4 3 2 1
176236—10/09

DK books are available at special discounts when purchased in bulk
for sales promotions, premiums, fund-raising, or educational use.
For details, contact: DK Publishing Special Markets,
375 Hudson Street, New York, New York 10014
SpecialSales@dk.com

A catalog record for this book is available from the Library of Congress.

ISBN: 978-0-7566-5772-7 (Paperback)
ISBN: 978-0-7566-5784-0 (Hardcover)

Color reproduction by Alta Image, UK
Printed and bound by L-Rex, China

Discover more at
www.dk.com

Contents

DK READERS

PROFICIENT

4

READERS

THE RISE OF
IRON MAN

Written by Michael Teitelbaum

Introduction

Tony Stark is a scientific genius, an amazing inventor, a brilliant businessman, and one of the richest men in the world. He is also the armor-clad Super Hero known as Iron Man.

It was clear from an early age that Tony was a genius. When he was seven years old, his wealthy parents sent him off to a boarding school. However, he was more interested in machines and how they worked than in making friends with the other children. By the time he was 15, Tony had been accepted at one of the best colleges in America. Four years later, he graduated at the top of his class. When Tony was 21, his parents were tragically killed in a car crash. Tony inherited their company called Stark Industries.

Business mind
Young Tony was not really interested in the family company. However, when he took over Stark Industries, he proved himself to be highly skilled in the world of business.

Great inventor
Tony is always
busy inventing
new gadgets
or improving
old ones.

After hours
At the end of
a busy day,
Tony likes to go
out to cool
nightclubs.

Stark Industries is a large company
that makes weapons for the military.
Even as head of Stark Industries,
Tony preferred his laboratory to the
boardroom and continued to invent
new things. One invention would
change Tony's life forever.

Large and small

Tony's inventions range from large items, like this aircraft carrier, to small things, such as a holo-communicator wristwatch that projects holograms.

Stark the inventor

The Starkworld Tech Conference takes place every year. Fans of the latest gadgets and computers attend this meeting. Each year, Tony reveals his latest invention.

One year, Tony unveiled a glider made of the lightest, sturdiest substance ever created. The substance is called Synth-Kinetic Interface Nano-fluid (S.K.I.N.).

The S.K.I.N. glider was powered by thermal uplifts and solar energy. Tony claimed that he would be the first person to fly around the Earth using powerless flight.

At the conference, inventor Dr. Ho Yinsen accused Tony of making weapons that had destroyed the country of Madripoor. Tony denied it, but Ho Yinsen's words upset him.

Tony took off in his glider, but a tornado threw the plane around. Tony crashed to the ground.

Dr. Ho Yinsen
Dr. Ho Yinsen was a brilliant and respected physicist, engineer, and professor. He did not believe in war and was against producing weapons.

Iron Man rising

When Tony awoke, he had been taken prisoner by agents of A.I.M. (Advanced Idea Mechanics). Tony learned that A.I.M. had been buying his company's weapons and using them to destroy Madripoor.

Tony was thrown into a high-tech lab filled with weapons and the remains of his S.K.I.N. glider. A.I.M. ordered him to build them an arsenal of weapons. They provided him with help—Dr. Yinsen himself, whom they had also kidnapped.

In secret, Tony and Yinsen used the S.K.I.N. material from the plane to build two suits of armor. They added weapons then donned the suits and blasted their way out. Yinsen did not survive, but Tony did and Iron Man was born.

A.I.M.
A.I.M. is an organization of brilliant scientists who are dedicated to gaining power and taking control of governments. Like Iron Man, Captain America has fought A.I.M.

Power
Iron Man's repulsor rays are his main weapons.

Armor-clad
Tony's Iron Man armor is lightweight to wear but completely indestructible.

Iron Man's armor

The original armor Tony built, while a prisoner of A.I.M., was just the first step in the development of the Iron Man battlesuit. Back in his laboratory, Tony perfected the suit, and added several new weapons and features.

Over many years of battling different Super Villains as Iron Man, Tony was able to develop a number of different types of armor. Each suit was designed for a special use, but all of the suits had elements in common.

The suit
Iron Man's armor protects him from attack and hides his true identity.

10

All of the suits are made of very strong but highly flexible materials. They all contain various weapons and a force field for added protection. Every suit gives Iron Man increased strength, the ability to fly, and a radar and communications system. Each suit contains a unibeam in the chest that acts as a spotlight as well as a laser, repulsor rays in the gloves, and jetboots.

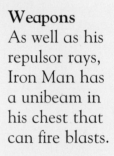

Weapons
As well as his repulsor rays, Iron Man has a unibeam in his chest that can fire blasts.

Jetboots
The jetboots in Iron Man's armor allow him to fly at great speeds.

Iron Man's suits include the stealth armor and the War Machine armor, which was worn by his friend James Rhodes.

Space armor
Iron Man's space armor is too heavy and bulky to use on Earth, but is perfect for use in outer space.

Specialized armor

Many of Iron Man's suits were built to cope with special situations. Some were built to battle specific beings. The space armor is extra strong to stand up to the pressures of operating in deep space. It has solar collectors to harness the sun's energy, and food and oxygen sources. It also has an external thruster to help Iron Man break free of Earth's gravitational pull.

Undersea armor
Iron Man's regular armor can operate underwater for short periods of time, but his underwater suit is better for longer missions.

Iron Man's undersea armor is leakproof and allows Iron Man to remain at the bottom of the ocean for long periods. Its weapons include manta ray torpedoes, an ink cloud like a squid's, and an electric field similar to an electric eel's.

Iron Man also made the Hulkbuster suit. He used it to fight the Hulk.

Hulkbuster armor
The Hulkbuster armor features enhanced strength and a very strong shell.

Tony's allies

As a businessman, Tony relies on his friends. Luckily, he has many.

Harold "Happy" Hogan was an unsuccessful boxer. When Tony was in a crash at a stock-car race, Hogan saved his life. A grateful Tony made Hogan his chauffeur.

Virginia "Pepper" Potts works at Stark Industries. When she corrected an error Tony had made, Tony made her his assistant. The pair care for each other, but their work relationship comes first.

Iron Man zooms in to rescues his loyal friends Happy Hogan and Pepper Potts.

Happy and Pepper
Both Happy and Pepper worked for Stark Industries. They soon fell in love with each other and married.

RHODES

Rhodey
Tony and
Rhodey met
when Rhodey
was a pilot in
the military.

James "Rhodey" Rhodes is Tony's
pilot and trusted ally. He wore Iron
Man's armor and filled in for Tony
when Tony had personal problems.
He has also battled various Super
Villains while wearing the War
Machine armor.

Edwin Jarvis is Tony's butler and
has been with the Stark family for
several years. When the Stark
mansion became the Avengers'
headquarters, Jarvis became butler
to the Super Hero team and
remained loyal to all its members.

Edwin Jarvis
Jarvis was a
pilot during
World War II.
After the war,
he went to
work as a butler
for Tony's
parents,
Howard and
Maria Stark, at
their mansion.

15

Iron Man's allies

Iron Man has teamed up with many Super Heroes. He has fought alongside them both on his own and as a member of the Super Hero group the Avengers.

The Hulk is a member of the Avengers and one of the strongest beings on Earth. The Hulk was created by a gamma ray blast. Iron Man has also fought the Hulk a few times, using his Hulkbuster armor.

The Hulk and Spider-Man
Both these heroes have teamed up with Iron Man many times, but they have also battled him.

Thor and Captain America
Thor and Captain America team up with Iron Man to make a tough trio.

Fantastic Four
The members of this Super Hero team have helped Iron Man using both their powers and their brilliant scientific knowledge.

Captain America is another of Iron Man's teammates in the Avengers. He was transformed to the peak of human perfection by a top secret Super-Soldier Serum. With Iron Man, he fights against Super Villains, alien invaders, and terrorists.

Nick Fury
Nick Fury is the director of S.H.I.E.L.D., a major anti-terrorist group. Iron Man helps Fury to work with Super Heroes.

Mandarin
A blast from one of Mandarin's rings can slam into Iron Man's unibeam.

Ten Rings
Each of Mandarin's Ten Rings has a different power.

Iron Man's enemies

Both Tony and Iron Man have had to battle many enemies foes over the years. They have all been tough enemies to beat.

Mandarin is a superpowered martial arts master and one of Iron Man's greatest enemies. Mandarin wears the Ten Rings of Power. They allow him to seize control of another being's mind, rearrange matter, and create fire, ice, electricity, and blinding bursts of light.

Stane's Iron Monger armor is loaded with weapons and gives him protection against attacks.

Tony's greatest foe is Obadiah Stane, a brilliant but ruthless businessman who tried to ruin Tony and take over Stark Industries. Stane also fought Iron Man as the armored Iron Monger.

Financial genius Justin Hammer tried to take over Tony's company. He used a high-tech device to gain control of Iron Man's armor. When Hammer used the armor to kill an ambassador, Iron Man was blamed, but Tony cleared his name.

Doctor Doom
Victor von
Doom is a great
scientist. As the
Super Villain
Doctor Doom,
he is a
dangerous foe
to Iron Man.

Further foes

Iron Man has battled with several
other dangerous Super Villains over
the years. These range from armored
villains to robots.

The Crimson Dynamo wears a
battlesuit similar to Iron Man's own.
This suit is loaded with weapons,
from missiles to guns, to electric
blast generators. Many enemies,
such as Crimson Dynamo, have
attempted to destroy Iron Man using
this type of technology.

Backlash

*Crimson
Dynamo*

Originally, Backlash was called Whiplash. He wore a battlesuit of steel mesh and a bulletproof cape. Justin Hammer later provided him with new weapons and armor, and he became Backlash.

Ultimo is a giant robot created by an alien race. The android was reprogrammed by Mandarin. Ultimo's aim is to destroy Iron Man. The two have fought many battles.

Titanium Man also wears armor like Iron Man's. His suit protects him from attacks, allows him to fly, and lets him fire energy blasts.

Madame Masque
When Whitney Frost's face was scarred during a raid on Stark Industries, she put on a golden mask and became Madam Masque.

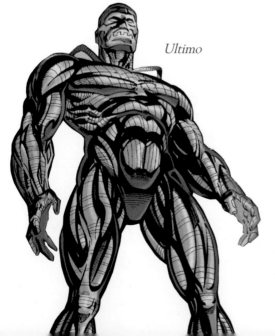

Ultimo

Titanium Man

Tony's loves

Tony has been in love on several occasions. Some of his girlfriends have worked for him at Stark Industries. Others started as Iron Man's enemies but switched sides later. All of them have one thing in common: They loved the billionaire businessman who became an armored Super Hero.

Bethany Cabe went to work for Tony as his bodyguard. She quickly fell in love with him. Bethany had been married before, but she believed that her husband had been killed in a car accident. She was shocked to find that her husband was still alive. Bethany promptly left Tony to help her husband. A faithful friend, she later returned to nurse Tony back to health when his personal problems became too much him.

Natasha Romanova was a Russian spy who used the code name "Black Widow." She hoped to steal Tony's technological secrets for the Russians. Hawkeye, a member of the Avengers, convinced Black Widow to change sides to America. Instead of stealing from Tony, she fell in love with him.

Black Widow
Black Widow is an expert at martial arts and a weapons specialist. Before she got her costume, she performed her spy missions in evening wear.

Maya Hansen
Scientist Maya Hansen was Tony's longtime friend. However, she betrayed Iron Man by letting her dangerous Extremis formula get into the hands of terrorists.

The Avengers

The Avengers is a Super Hero team whose lineup has changed over the years. Through the changes, Iron Man has remained one of the Avengers' staunchest supporters and even its leader at times.

Iron Man never meant to be in a team. However, when the evil Loki tried to trick the Hulk into causing a train wreck, Iron Man joined with Thor, Ant-Man, and Wasp.

Lineup
In addition to well-known heroes, the Avengers has consisted of supernatural beings, humans, robots, and aliens.

Loki
Loki cannot read the minds of others, but he can control their actions.

The heroes decided to stop the Hulk. When they realized that Loki had tricked them, they came together to stop him. Ant-Man suggested they remain a team and Wasp came up with the name. The Avengers was born.

The team have kept going. This is largely due to Tony's technical genius, the equipment and resources of Stark Industries, and the power of Iron Man.

Other Avengers
Over the years other members of the Avengers team have included Ronin, Luke Cage, Spider-Woman, Sentry, Spider-Man, Wolverine, and Captain America.

The Avengers battle superhuman and alien threats wherever they appear.

25

**Director of
S.H.I.E.L.D.**
Nick Fury's
combat
experience and
his Super Hero
contacts made
him the perfect
choice to be the
Director of
S.H.I.E.L.D.

S.H.I.E.L.D.

S.H.I.E.L.D. stands for Supreme
Headquarters International
Espionage Law-enforcement
Division. This anti-terrorism
organization often needs help from
Iron Man and the Avengers.

S.H.I.E.L.D. was formed mainly to
deal with threats from superhumans.
It was set up by the US government.

World War II commando Nick Fury was selected to lead the highly skilled and well-armed group of S.H.I.E.L.D. agents. Captain America, Spider-Woman, and Iron Man have all served as S.H.I.E.L.D. agents, and the entire Avengers team is often called on to assist the organization. Fury has also had to ask for help from other Super Heroes, like the Fantastic Four, on more than one occasion.

Headquarters
S.H.I.E.L.D.'s base is on a huge aircraft called the Helicarrier. It was created by Stark Industries.

Iron Man and Fury discuss a top-secret project that Tony is funding.

A new Iron Man

It seems that Tony has a perfect life. He is a rich businessman, and, as Iron Man, he is a powerful Super Hero. However, Tony has many foes who envy him and want to ruin him.

Iron Man had always supported S.H.I.E.L.D. until he found out the agency was secretly buying parts of Stark Industries. The group hoped to take over Stark Industries and get the company to make weapons just for the group.

At the same time, Obadiah Stane tricked Tony into losing control of Stark Industries. Devastated, Tony was unable to act as Iron Man.

Luckily, Tony's close friend James Rhodes was around to help. Rhodey put on the Iron Man armor and took his friend's place. Tony started to put his life back together, but Rhodey began to go mad. Tony realized that Rhodey could not use the armor for long periods of time because it was designed just for Tony. Tony used a magnetic lock to shut down the armor and save his friend.

Armored friend
Rhodey's War Machine armor is solar-charged. Like Iron Man's armor, it has a powerful unibeam.

Scarlet Witch
Scarlet Witch is a member of the Avengers and Force Works. She has incredible mental powers.

Spider-Woman
Spider-Woman can stick to walls, has great strength, and can fly.

Force Works

Iron Man decided to leave the Avengers just as another Super Hero team called the West Coast Avengers split up.

Iron Man joined up with some of the former West Coast Avengers to form a new group, which he called Force Works.

The other members of this new team were Scarlet Witch, US Agent, Wonder Man, and Spider-Woman. An alien called Century and War Machine also joined the group, but soon left when they came into conflict with Iron Man.

Force Works battled many aliens, such as the Kree.

The team also had adventures around the world. Eventually the group split up. The members went their separate ways and Iron Man returned to the Avengers.

US Agent
US Agent has superhuman strength. He carries an indestructible shield made of Vibranium.

Wonder Man
Wonder Man is as strong as Thor. He flies using a jet flight-pack.

Kang the Conqueror
Kang battled Iron Man and the Avengers right from the team's formation.

Death and Rebirth

For several years, the time traveler Kang the Conqueror controlled Tony's mind. Kang forced Iron Man to kill many individuals, including some of his Avengers teammates.

The remaining Avengers traveled back in time. They recruited a young Tony to return with them and fight the adult Tony and Kang.

Stealing a suit of Tony's Iron Man armor, teenage Tony engaged in battle with adult Tony. During this struggle, adult Tony remembered all the individuals who he had been forced to kill and broke free of Kang's mind control. Tony destroyed Kang and sacrificed himself in the battle.

One Iron Man battling another Iron Man means double the trouble!

Teen Tony stayed in the present and teamed up with the Avengers to battle the evil mutant Onslaught. During this battle, teen Tony was killed, along with his fellow Avengers and the Fantastic Four. Fortunately, Franklin Richards, son of Sue and Reed Richards from the Fantastic Four, had created a pocket universe, which was used to restore adult Tony's life and the life of the other heroes.

Franklin Richards held the key to saving the lives of the Avengers.

Onslaught
Onslaught was formed when Professor X's and Magneto's minds clashed. It has Professor X's mental skills and Magneto's magnetic powers.

Ultron
Ultron was built as a servant but this superpowered robot gained a mind of its own.

Stark versus Iron Man

Tony's Iron Man armor has always been his most valuable tool. But what if the armor came alive and had a mind of its own? This is exactly what happened!

Tony tried to save an android by downloading its programming into his Iron Man suit. However, he did not know that the evil robot Ultron had embedded himself in the android's system. As a result, when the Super Villain Whiplash sent a shock into the Iron Man armor, Tony suffered a heart attack. That shock also awakened the armor and gave it a mind of its own.

A powerful electric shock from Whiplash almost kills Iron Man.

When his battlesuit comes alive, Iron Man is forced to fight himself.

The armor realized that Tony had suffered a heart attack. It quickly ripped out some of its own parts and built a cybernetic heart that saved Tony's life. However, when the armor tried to force Tony to merge with it, he knew he had to fight it.

The human Tony had no chance of defeating the powerful armor he had built. During the fight, Tony suffered another heart attack. This time the armor decided to save Tony's life by sacrificing itself.

Whiplash
Whiplash wears a bulletproof cape and is an expert at martial arts and hand-to-hand combat.

Tony watches in amazement as his Iron Man armor is ruined.

Avengers disassembled

"Avengers assemble" is the battle cry used to gather the Avengers team together. However, when the Scarlet Witch went insane, the team was forced to disassemble.

The Scarlet Witch is a mutant who can alter reality. Usually the Scarlet Witch can control this power, but when she went insane, she lost control. She manipulated Tony into saying that the country of Latveria should be destroyed.

Tony then announced that the Avengers were breaking up.

He knew that people did not trust him because of his remarks about Latveria. He said that someone else would be wearing his armor. Tony hoped this would stop people from mistrusting Iron Man. However, he secretly continued to be Iron Man.

A new group of Super Heroes came together to continue the Avengers' work. This team is called the New Avengers.

The New Avengers, including Spider-Man, Spider-Woman, and Wolverine, burst into action.

Stark Tower
When the Scarlet Witch destroyed the Avengers' mansion, Tony built Stark Tower. This became the New Avengers' base.

Professor X
Professor
Charles Xavier
is a mutant
with incredible
mental powers.
He fights for
mutant-human
equality and
cooperation.

Doctor Strange
Doctor Strange
can probe the
minds of others
and has a cloak
of levitation
that allows
him to fly.

The Illuminati

Following the long war between the alien races known as the Kree and the Skrulls, Iron Man decided to form a new secret organization called the Illuminati. He hoped that the combined knowledge and abilities of the team's members would be able to prevent wars in the future.

Iron Man brought together some of the most important Super Heroes. Each member represented a different group of individuals.

The powerful Illuminati hope to prevent future wars and tragedies.

Iron Man represented the government. Mr. Fantastic stood for the scientific community while Prince Namor, the Sub-Mariner, represented the seas. Professor X, the leader of the X-Men, was the representative of the mutant community, and Black Bolt stood for the Inhumans. Doctor Strange, Master of the Mystic Arts, represented the magical community.

However, the Illuminati became divided because some members started to distrust each other. Ultimately, the Illuminati split up.

When Prince Namor disagreed with the Illuminati, Iron Man tried to convince him otherwise. The pair ended up fighting over it.

Black Bolt
This Inhuman can trigger shock waves, create force fields, and has superhuman strength.

Mr. Fantastic
Mr. Fantastic is a scientist and can stretch his body. He got his powers from cosmic radiation.

Civil war

The American government had been considering passing an act called the Superhuman Registration Act. This would mean that every superhuman would have to register with the government. The debate over this act would lead to a civil war among the Super Heroes.

Some heroes were for the act while others were against it. At first, Iron Man was unhappy with it. He believed it would take away superhumans' privacy.

Nitro
Nitro can cause his body to explode, then can reform it at will.

Waiting game
Happy Hogan and Tony wait to hear if the registration act has been passed.

Iron Man's view changed when members of a Super Hero team called the New Warriors confronted Super Villain Nitro in a crowded neighborhood. The battle ended when Nitro caused a massive explosion. Many innocent people died. From this point on, Iron Man was in favor of the registration act.

The act was passed but the Super Heroes were still divided about the issue. The two sides battled in a civil war. The Super Heroes who had fought alongside each other were now fighting against each other.

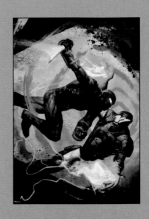

New Warriors
The New Warriors do not always see eye to eye with Iron Man.

Brutal battle
The civil war saw Super Hero fight Super Hero. Even Captain America and Iron Man clashed during the huge conflict.

World war Hulk

The Illuminati were concerned about the Hulk. They believed that the Hulk's outbursts were a threat to the safety of Earth.

Blasted off!
The Illuminati agreed that the only way to save Earth from the Hulk was to blast him into space.

So, Iron Man and the team tricked the Hulk into entering a spaceship and launched it to another planet. Some time later, the Hulk returned to Earth and vowed to get his revenge on the Illuminati. Iron Man was the first hero to confront the angry Hulk. Tony realized his armor would not stand up to the Hulk.

When Iron Man donned his Hulkbuster armor, the Hulk put on some new armor of his own.

42

Hulkbuster armor

Tony created the new Hulkbuster armor. It is a shell that fits around Iron Man's normal armor. The gloves are rocket-boosted and can hit the Hulk with a mighty punch.

Instead, he put on specially designed Hulkbuster armor.

However, Iron Man's new armor was no match for the power of the Hulk and the Hulk destroyed the armor. Iron Man fought back and used a satellite to hit Hulk with a gamma blast, which knocked him unconscious and ended the battle.

Battle damage
The huge fight between the Hulk and Iron Man ruined the city. Even Stark Tower was destroyed.

Secret invasion

In the world of Super Heroes and Villains, it is not easy to tell who you can trust. Iron Man found this out quickly.

Elektra
When Elektra died, her true identity was revealed. This Elektra was actually a Skrull.

Elektra, leader of the group of ninja assassins known as The Hand, was killed in battle with the New Avengers. However, it emerged that the being who seemed to be Elektra was actually a shapeshifting Skrull.

The New Avengers were shocked and wondered if any of their members might also be Skrulls.

The Skrulls are an alien race who are determined to invade Earth. They can change their appearance, which is known as shapeshifting.

They also worried that the Skrulls might be invading Earth.

Iron Man was the first of the New Avengers to be suspected of being a Skrull. Spider-Woman showed him the Skrull's body. If Iron Man was a Skrull, he would react to seeing another one. However, it was clear that Iron Man was not a Skrull.

When Tony showed the Skrull's body to the Illuminati, it was a different story. It revealed that Black Bolt was a Skrull. As the Skrull's secret invasion got more serious, the New Avengers teamed up with S.H.I.E.L.D. to put an end to it.

Shapeshifting Using their abilities, the Skrulls can make themselves look like any individual they want.

Dark reign

Iron Man was forced to step down as leader of S.H.I.E.L.D. and the Avengers because he failed to stop the Skrull's secret invasion. He was replaced by Norman Osborn, Spider-Man's greatest enemy. Osborn joined with some powerful but evil allies and formed the secret society called the Cabal. Iron Man was now on the run.

No one knows what is next for Iron Man. Only time will tell if he will take his place again as one of the world's greatest Super Heroes.

Fugitive
After the secret invasion, the once great hero became a wanted man.

Thinking time
Iron Man will need to work hard to win back people's trust and respect.

Glossary

aftermath
A period following an event.

ambassador
A representative of a government in another country.

android
A robot.

arsenal
A collection, usually of weapons.

boarding school
A private school where students live and study together.

butler
A male servant who takes care of all the needs of a household.

chauffeur
A person employed to drive a car.

commando
A member of a military unit.

cybernetic
Artificial or mechanical.

disassemble
To break apart.

donned
Put on.

embedded
Placed in.

espionage
To do with spying.

flexible
Easily bendable.

force field
A barrier made of energy to protect someone.

gamma ray
Radiation of high energy.

graduated
Having completed college with a degree.

gravitational pull
The power of Earth's gravity.

holograms
Three-dimensional images.

levitation
The act of rising or floating in the air.

manipulated
Controlled or influenced.

mistrusting
Not trusting.

mutant
A non-human who is born with special abilities.

registration
The act of listing or keeping records about something.

repulsor
Something that forces a thing back.

solar
To do with the sun.

staunchest
Strongest.

stock-car race
A race using cars that are similar to passenger cars.

sturdiest
The thing that is built the strongest.

thermal
To do with heat.

tornado
A violent windstorm.

uplifts
The act of raising something up.

ecofaith

ecofaith

creating & sustaining
green congregations

CHARLENE HOSENFELD

THE
PILGRIM
PRESS
Cleveland

To our planet
and all who are committed
to her care

The Pilgrim Press
700 Prospect Avenue
Cleveland, Ohio 44115-1100
thepilgrimpress.com

Printed in the United States of America on acid-free paper

14 13 12 11 10 09   5 4 3 2

Library of Congress Cataloging-in-Publication Data

Hosenfeld, Charlene A., 1950-
    Ecofaith : creating and sustaining green congregations / Charlene
Hosenfeld.
        p. cm.
    Includes bibliographical references and index.
    ISBN 978-0-8298-1818-5 (alk. paper)
    1. Human ecology – Religious aspects – Christianity. 2. Stewardship,
Christian. 3. Environmental ethics.   I. Title.
BT695.5.H67 2009
261.8′8 – dc22

                                                        2008041157

Contents

Acknowledgments

Many people are part of the process of creating a book. I want to thank those who helped me in the three-year process of bringing *Eco-Faith* from just an idea to a reality. From our first conversation in June 2006 about the need for a book on the topic of greening churches, my friend and colleague the Rev. Dr. Andrew Weaver was clear in his message to me: it is a good idea; you *should* do it. A year later, Rev. Carolyn Stapleton was clear in her message to me when I was unsure even how to approach the project; you *can* do it. And so I began to write a proposal for the book.

I am grateful for the staff at The Pilgrim Press for accepting my proposal and for publishing the book. Kim Sadler helped me understand that a handbook format would be the most user-friendly for the reader, and Joan Blake was unfailingly enthusiastic and supportive.

I extend a special thanks to my editor, Ulrike Guthrie, whose skill and sharp eye improved my work.

The environmental stewards who shared with me their accounts of their congregations' green actions for the "Inspiring Stories" section of the book were terrific. These folks and the others who work alongside them are literally making all the difference in the world. Special thanks go to Father Charles Morris, Rev. Amy Bowden Freedman, Wailani Robins, Bill Breakey, Allison Fisher, Lina Parikh, and Patricia McBee.

I am very grateful for the efforts of my fellow members of Christ Church Uniting in Kailua, on the island of Oʻahu, for their continuing efforts to green our church and our lives. We have a core Green Team, but I think of our entire small but powerful congregation as being the team. A special *mahalo* though to Pastor Buddy Sommers, Estelle Codier, Ann Bell, Beth Davidann, John Heidel, Marian Heidel, Connie Mitchell, Mark Mitchell, Melody Heidel, Jane Muench, and Paul Belanger.

At the time of this writing, I am looking forward to attending the Climate Project's first Faith Community Training. Thanks to Al Gore for his incredible work in bringing the issue of global warming to light through film, print, and trainings. He has awakened the green hearts of many. By the time you read this, trainees will be spreading the word even further in faith communities. Contact the Climate Project (*www.theclimateproject.org*) to schedule a presentation for your group.

I also want to thank my friends and family for their support through the long process from conception of the book to its completion. Especially I thank Bonnie Chan and Linda Pickenpaugh, who both were unwavering in their support and encouragement. And I thank my husband, Rollo Scheurenbrand. I know now what people mean when they say, "I couldn't have done it without him."

Most of all, I want to thank all of you who are reading *Eco-Faith* and putting your faith into action. *Every action matters.*

Introduction

Eco-Faith: Creating and Sustaining Green Congregations is intended to be a user-friendly guide to help pastors, church leaders, congregations, and individuals understand environmental issues as they relate to caring for the whole of God's creation. *Eco-Faith* draws on extensive resources and cites many specific references.

I wrote this book because I am passionate about environmental stewardship, totally convinced that we must make major changes in order to protect the Earth and all its inhabitants, and because I believe that people of religious faith are a natural fit for leadership in this effort: they are dedicated to social justice and caring for others, and they are grateful for the gifts of God. What greater gift than the Earth that is home to us all? Environmental stewardship — protecting and nurturing the Earth and all the life it sustains — is after all not only an environmental issue or a political issue, but a moral issue. As such, it is a perfect fit for religious people and faith communities. People of faith have historically emerged from behind their church doors to take significant roles in fighting against social injustice and fighting for justice. Slavery, poverty, civil rights, and hunger are but a few of the issues that have prompted religious responses. The addition of Earth-justice to churches' social-justice agendas is logical, timely, and necessary.

Eco-Faith focuses on *awareness* of problems, the *interconnectedness* of everything, *skills* and practices to learn, and *actions* to take. It incorporates solid ecological science with sound theology and with related research-based psychology. I am a psychologist by profession, and so I recognize the importance of addressing the psychological aspects of the human–nature connection and of effecting behavior change. Inclusion of the psychological perspective is a unique aspect of this book. Indeed, *Eco-Faith* synthesizes information from a wide range of scientific, theological, and psychological sources, and provides suggestions for ways to adopt environmental stewardship practices within the context of religious life. Though the integration of the three areas is vital, I briefly address each one separately in the Appendix. The psychology section summarizes the contribution of psychology to the understanding of human behavior in relation to the environment. This section deals with how best to implement pro-environment changes with your congregation to maximize your chances of getting good results.

Readers who want to gain knowledge about global warming, pollution, environmental degradation, related social issues (such as poverty and hunger), and the relationship of these topics to religious faith and practice can read the theology and ecology sections for specific information and a review of the connections between these. However readers who want only the "ways" to start or increase environmental or green stewardship practices in their church and individual lives can limit their reading to the chapters in Part One of the book that provide suggestions for practical, doable actions. Each of these chapters can stand alone, though some are interwoven and complementary. Each action section in the chapters suggests large and small steps that individual readers or a congregation can take on behalf of environmental stewardship. Taken together, they comprise a holistic plan of church-related environmental stewardship.

Psychological research indicates that when people feel overwhelmed by a problem or task, they are not motivated to take action. Our environmental crisis can certainly be overwhelming.

Eco-Faith focuses on doable actions so that readers can be empowered, not overwhelmed. A theme that runs throughout the book is that *every action matters* and can make a positive difference at the human, planet, and spirit levels. Actual stories of changes and successes from churches of varied denominations, size, ethnic and cultural composition, and geographical locations punctuate that theme. The synergistic effect of combining people of faith with environmental stewardship is abundantly evident in these stories.

Psychological research also provides information about why environmental stewardship is important to healthy human functioning, and about how best to encourage people to engage in environmentally friendly practices. See the psychology section of the Appendix (page 183 below) for proven strategies and tools to use when designing and implementing church-based environmental programs.

Part One, which follows this Introduction, is divided into seven chapters and focuses on specific action areas: the Building, the Grounds, Products, Worship and Services, Finances, Children's Activities, and Special Projects. Each of these chapter sections includes: a brief **Introduction, Facts** (a list of topic-related information), **Actions** (specific steps to take), and **Resources** (a list of books, websites, and other resources from which the Facts information was gathered, and which suggest further sources of related information). The Resources sections are especially important because readers will no doubt want to explore some topics further.

A vast and sometimes daunting amount of information is available on the Internet, and numerous websites are listed in the Resources sections. According to the United Nations statistics database (2008), an estimated 69 percent of people in the United States access the Internet, and this number continues to grow each year. Internet resources are an essential part of *Eco-Faith,* and they provide up-to-date information for the reader. I have included websites that I have found to be particularly relevant, interesting, and helpful, and from which I gathered information. I have checked and rechecked the addresses to ensure that they do in fact link to the resources listed. However websites, content, and addresses (URLs) do change, so if you find one that does not link correctly, try a shortened version of the address — e.g., *www.*[the organization name or initials].*org* or .*com*. If this locates the website, then use the "search" function or tabs on the website to find a specific article or fact.

Part Two focuses on inspiring stories of churches from around the country and features actual and inspiring environmentally responsible actions implemented by congregations. Having the opportunity to speak with the people involved in the greening of these divergent churches and congregations was for me a privilege and a highlight of writing *Eco-Faith*.

The **Appendix** is a discussion of environment-related theology, psychology, and ecology, and the interrelationship of the three. There are separate lists of **Recommended Readings** for those interested in furthering their knowledge of these topics as they relate to the contents of the book.

THEOLOGY, PSYCHOLOGY, AND ECOLOGY

Religious faith, psychological well-being, and environmental stewardship are interconnected. One without the other two is insufficient for the task at hand. *Eco-Faith: Creating and Sustaining Green Congregations* is a blend of all three. Our task is no less than reversing the human degradation of our planet and mobilizing people of faith to become people of action in caring for God's creation.

As a psychologist in private practice, I help people identify and change personal maladaptive patterns of thinking and behaving. *Awareness* is the first step in making personal change. This is a necessary step, but far from sufficient. Also necessary is understanding the emotional, cognitive, and behavioral impact of one's past experiences, and the *connections* between these. This understanding can help a person determine what personal changes in thinking and actions would be beneficial. Learning the *skills* to transform thoughts, feelings, and actions is then vital to effect personal change. Having the motivation and *commitment* to change and to make choices that support psychological health is not always easy, but in the long run it is worth the effort.

Awareness and understanding of interconnectedness are also necessary components of linking religious faith to environmental stewardship. Many writers from many different faith traditions have made the case for a spiritual link to Earth care. This book focuses on Christianity only because that is the religious tradition with which I am most familiar. The theology section in the Appendix discusses the biblical mandate for environmental stewardship and provides a summary of some of the related denominational policies and statements. In stunningly strong, often poetic, and always clear voices, church leaders continue to call their members to action — individual, social, congregational, and even political action. So far we have answered these calls to action in a limited way. A groundswell of action at the local church level has not yet occurred, but I believe it is imminent. The purpose of this book is to fuel such a groundswell of action.

When I first began researching the various denominational positions and statements on caring for the environment, I was truly amazed at what I found. The breadth and clarity of the statements was remarkable, as was the fact that many were written fifteen or twenty years ago. The link between being a Christian and caring for the environment is articulated repeatedly in denominational statements, programs, and curricula, and in faith–environment books and websites. Topics range from global warming and decreasing energy use to less publicized environmental stewardship topics such as family farming, toxic dumps, paper use, air quality, strip mining, oil drilling in the Arctic, water quality, and mountaintop removal coal mining. Amazing thinkers showing great leadership. This information has been slowly percolating down through the decades and the denominational bureaucracies. Our job now is to act on these calls to action.

INTERCONNECTEDNESS

Once one perceives the link between Christian faith and environmental stewardship, then *developing awareness* (of environmental problems and of the connections between all of the Earth, all living beings, and all of our actions) is the first step toward making necessary eco-faith changes. The next step, as in personal change, is *learning skills* — in this case learning ways to transform environmentally irresponsible actions into Earth-respecting actions. Finally, we must *make a commitment to change and* to *take action* to nurture and restore the Earth. This is where psychological research enters the picture by providing information about ways to best effect pro-environment changes in people.

We are not apart from, but we are a part of the Earth — and all the land, water, air, vegetation, and creatures (human and otherwise) it sustains. As such, we are responsible for caring for all that is joined in the intricate web of life. Everything is connected. Once we know that from our very core, we truly know that every action matters.

Understanding interconnectedness is fundamental to being a Christian and to being an environmental steward. Every time we give food to those who have little or donate money to mission work, we are aware of our connection to others. Every time we turn off lights or unplug appliances that are not being used, we are aware of our connection to the natural resources of the planet. Every time we enjoy the beauty of a mountain or flower, we are aware of our connection to nature. And every time we work or play together, we are aware of our connection to each other. We are indeed a part of the Earth. When we harm the Earth, we harm ourselves. And when we heal the Earth, we heal ourselves.

To participate in this healing and to make the vital (though sometimes difficult or inconvenient) changes in our actions, we need to think wholistically, long-term, and interconnectedly. Since everything is interconnected, the work to be done is interpersonal, interfaith, and international. The more we recognize ourselves as being part of the whole, the easier it becomes to think and act in terms of the "common good" and consider the impact of our every action on others. What is good for one's personal health and well-being is good for the health and well-being of the entire planet. Common-good thinking facilitates environmental stewardship.

MAKING CHANGES

In the big picture, necessary changes include increasing vehicle fuel efficiency and decreasing vehicle use, making buildings more efficient, decreasing fossil fuel energy use and increasing use of renewable sources of power, eliminating tropical deforestation and increasing new tree plantations, and using and supporting sustainable farming methods (Gravitz 2006; Intergovernmental Panel on Climate Change [IPCC] 2007c; United Nations 2006).

In the smaller picture of our day-to-day lives we can take action and make many changes that will reduce our footprint on the Earth. Taking action serves to mitigate feelings of hopelessness about the enormity of the problem. When we feel overwhelmed by the task at hand, taking action and making positive change is the antidote. No Earth-friendly action is too small, though massive and immediate steps by large numbers of people are needed to effect the necessary global changes. This is where *Eco-Faith* comes into the picture. I envision people of faith stepping up to the plate — in small and quiet ways and in huge and public ways; in tiny churches and in mega-churches; in rural areas, small towns, suburbs, and cities; and across all denominational, socio-economic, racial, and ethnic lines.

Psychological research has shown us that individual behavior change is more likely to occur once the desired behavior is the usual and accepted practice — i.e., it becomes the norm. As we make individual changes and model environmentally responsible behavior, we are not only doing our part for the environment, we are helping to change societal norms. And as more people engage in environmentally responsible behaviors, more people will join them.

Following are some personal behavior change recommendations:

- Drive less and use public transportation more.

- Walk or bike for short trips.

- Drive a fuel-efficient vehicle.

- Insulate well.

- Install solar attic fans.

- Turn your air-conditioning off or to a higher temperature.

- Turn your heat down.

- Use compact florescent lights and turn them off when they are not needed.

- Think before you buy.

- Buy less.

- Buy quality products that will last, not cheap products that rapidly end up in the landfill.

- Turn off your computer when you are not using it.

- Plug electronic equipment into power strips and turn the power strips off when the equipment is not in use.

- Hang laundry outside to dry by the sun and wind instead of using fossil fuels.

- Buy only energy efficient appliances.

- Install a solar hot water system.

- Use dual flush and very low flush toilets.

- Take shorter showers.

- Support local farmers and those who use sustainable farming methods.

- Buy organic food and clothing made from natural and organic fabrics to decrease toxic chemicals in our ecosystem.

- Compost.

- Avoid wood, food, and coffee products that contribute to tropical forest destruction.

- Eat less meat.

- Choose glass over plastic, and recycle.

- Buy in bulk when possible and use refillable containers.

- Carry small purchases without bags, and take reusable shopping bags to the store.

- Take your own reusable cup or mug to the coffee shop, fast food restaurant, and work.

- Take your own container to the bakery or carry-out food restaurant.

- Avoid disposable razors, pens, utensils, and cups.

- Use, wash, and reuse cloth rags and napkins.

- Travel with your reusable bags and mugs.

- Write letters to companies asking that they find alternatives to excessive packaging.

- Stop junk mail, unwanted catalogs, and credit card offers.

- Make your own nontoxic and Earth-friendly cleaning products and store them in reusable containers.

- Make Earth-friendly changes so that green practices eventually become the norm.

- Read *Eco-Faith*.

- Be involved in environmental stewardship actions at your church.

Eco-Faith = People of faith
becoming people of green action.

Awareness — Interconnectedness — Commitment — Action

Every action matters

PART ONE

Action Steps

Chapter One

The Building

A place of worship is far more than a building. However, the building is a good place to start when we look for ways to save energy and to become good stewards of the environment. Any changes we make that decrease energy use are steps in the right direction. Once we become attuned to recognizing where energy is being wasted, we see many examples; once we become aware of energy waste, we can make changes. In addition, we can reduce our energy *needs* and shift to renewable sources. As we rethink energy use, we can also rethink and then reduce water use. And we can extend the rethinking approach to the paper and other products we use, and to the ways we generate and dispose of waste. The mantra "Rethink, Reduce, Reuse, Recycle" is succinct and eminently useful.

I address many aspects of church building structure and practices in this section: assessment of the building's current energy use, what to consider when planning and building a new structure or when renovating an old one, ways to reduce energy consumption (and possibly even to become "carbon neutral"), kinds of equipment to use, ways to reduce paper use, and what and how to recycle. All have one thing in common: when we make good choices related to these things, we save energy. And when we use less fossil fuel energy, we contribute less to global warming.

Global warming, and the resulting climate change, is arguably the most important issue of our time. It affects *all* life on Earth.

However, of particular interest to people of faith, whose mission work is often related to poverty issues, is that poor communities are especially vulnerable to the negative effects of climate change (Christian Aid 2008; IPCC 2007c; Presbyterian Church USA 2007; World Council of Churches 2007). These communities have limited adaptive capabilities and are more dependent on climate-sensitive resources such as local water and food supplies (IPCC 2007c). When water becomes scarce or contaminated and farmlands are no longer viable, then greater poverty, hunger, and illness result. Humans and the Earth as a whole suffer. And so global warming is a moral and not just a political issue (Gore 2006; Sleeth 2006). And the multitude of religious groups now focused on the issue indicates that it is clearly also a spiritual issue. I believe it is most useful to conceptualize global warming as all-inclusive — as a political, moral, spiritual, psychological, and physical health issue. We have personal and collective responsibility to take action.

Global warming and its far-reaching effects are the result of carbon dioxide (CO_2) and other greenhouse gases (GHGs) in the atmosphere. Anthropogenic (human-caused) GHG emissions are mainly due to the burning of fossil fuels, deforestation, and agricultural activities. These gases build up in the atmosphere and create a barrier that traps heat over the Earth. The average American creates approximately five times the average carbon emissions per person worldwide (Earth Policy Institute 2008; Sierra 2006). It is time and it is our responsibility to significantly reduce our emissions.

One way to do this is to assess our church buildings and our practices within (and outside) these buildings, and to make changes as needed and possible. "Greening" a building means evaluating current conditions and practices, then taking steps — small and large — to reduce the use of greenhouse-gas-causing fossil fuels that contribute to global warming. We can green both the structure and the practices of the sanctuary, office, kitchen, bathrooms, and other building spaces.

Changes can be small and easy (e.g., turning out lights), or they can be large and complex (switching from fossil-fuel-produced electricity to renewable forms of energy). Changes can be direct (replacing incandescent light bulbs with compact fluorescents) or indirect (buying high quality office equipment instead of cheaper, but short-lived, landfill-bound equipment). Some green building-related practices are well-known (recycling aluminum cans), and some have received far less attention (e-waste disposal). I considered not even including the topic of recycling beverage cans in this book because it is such a well known practice, but then I learned that the 2006 recycling rate for aluminum cans was only about 50 percent — lower even than the rate in the 1990s. This means that an estimated 48 billion cans were thrown in landfills or along highways or were burned in incinerators in 2006 (Spillman 2008). And this is aluminum — one of the truly recyclable products and one that almost everyone knows can be recycled. Making a new aluminum can from an old one uses 90–95 percent less energy than making a totally new can and is, of course, the thing to do. The can is then no longer "waste," but a *resource*. With only about one-half of all cans being recycled, we obviously need to help facilitate a societal change of habits. This we can do. Many churches across the nation are already recycling — and many are doing far more. They are making remarkable changes to green their buildings, their practices, and their actions. See "Inspiring Stories..." in Part Two — they are indeed inspiring.

Reducing energy and water use saves money, decreases the amount of pollution and greenhouse gases (GHGs) generated, and decreases our contribution to global warming. This chapter provides a summary of related Facts, suggestions for Actions, and a list of Resources for each action. Read on....

BUILD AND REMODEL GREEN

Facts

* Buildings have an enormous impact on the environment.

* In the United States, buildings account for 70 percent of electricity use, 39 percent of total energy use, 39 percent of carbon emissions, 40 percent of raw material use, 30 percent of waste generated, and 12 percent of potable water use (U.S. Green Building Council, 2008).

* A green building is designed to reduce negative impacts on the environment and on health throughout the *entire lifetime* of the building — from site choice and design to construction, renovation, and demolition.

* A green building has multiple benefits according to the EPA:

  Environmental benefits:

  > protects ecosystems

  > reduces air and water pollution

  > reduces waste

  > conserves natural resources

  Economic benefits:

  > qualifies for incentives and funding

  > reduces operating costs

  > supports expansion of green products and services

  > maximizes the lifecycle of the building

  Social benefits:

  > eliminates toxic products and protects occupant health

  > reduces strain on the local infrastructure

  > enhances aesthetics

- Environmentally friendly building design and materials are available.

- Existing buildings can be greened in varying degrees or in stages through remodeling, retrofitting, and improving systems.

- Any remodeling or new construction can be viewed with a green eye.

- Some architects and contractors specialize in green design and construction.

- Green building is a rapidly growing segment of the construction market, supported by government programs, professionals in the field, business and homeowner interest, incentives, and common sense.

- Churches are joining this trend.

Actions

- *Research* the topic and form a building committee to oversee all related decisions.

- *Talk with others* in your area who have been involved in green building projects.

- *Contract* with an architect, builder, and subcontractors who have a commitment to using environmentally friendly designs, materials, and practices.

- *Sell, donate, or otherwise responsibly recycle* usable materials from any demolition.

- *Choose a building design* appropriate to your particular needs and one that considers:

  > siting of the project to protect the ecosystem

  > energy and water efficiency

> use of local materials and products

> shade and sun exposure

> placement of windows for natural views, light, breezes, and heat and air conditioning retention

> storm water runoff management

> landscaping that suits the climate conditions

- *Incorporate renewable energy systems* (e.g., solar hot water, photovoltaic panels, wind turbines, pellet furnace) as possible.

- *Consider the "true cost"* of all choices — not just the financial cost. Take into account the conditions under which products are produced and manufactured, their durability and expected lifespan, their content and source of the materials as well as their toxicity and associated health risks, and the distance products have to be transported.

- *Use products and materials sourced locally* when possible.

- *Reuse* others' discarded materials when possible by purchasing them from architectural salvage companies.

- *Use reclaimed wood* when possible.

- *Use material with recycled content* (e.g., insulation, tile).

- *Use Forest Stewardship Council (FSC) certified* wood.

- *Use the greenest available* flooring, paint, finishes, adhesives, bathroom fixtures, and kitchen fixtures and appliances.

Resources

- BuildingGreen LLC, *www.buildinggreen.com*. This company offers print and online information and resources "to help you design and build construction projects from a whole-systems perspective and take an integrated design approach that minimizes ecological impact and maximizes economic performance." The website provides a well-organized and easy-to-use directory of over two thousand "environmentally preferable products," with articles and links. Access to the full content of the website requires a paid membership of ($199/year; however, a very inexpensive one-week membership is also available.

- Construction Materials Recycling Association (CMRA), P.O. Box 122, Eola, IL 60519; (630) 585-7530; online at *www.cdrecycling.org*. CMRA promotes recycling of construction and demolition materials. The website provides a state-by-state listing of recyclers.

- Environmental Protection Agency (EPA) Green Building, *www.epa.gov/greenbuilding*. This comprehensive website provides information about a wide range of green building topics including energy and water efficiency, renewable energy, toxic waste reduction, indoor air quality, storm water management, and green roofs. The site provides information about funding of green building projects, as well as links to relevant federal, state, local, and utility programs including grants, loans, tax credits, and rebates. The EPA Industrial Materials Recycling Program provides information about how construction and demolition debris can be recycled, the Environmentally Preferable Purchasing Program includes information on building products, and the Office of Solid Waste addresses the reduction, reuse, and recycling of waste from construction, renovation, and demolition.

- Forest Stewardship Council (FSC), *www.fscus.org*. This organization accredits independent certifiers to evaluate and certify forests using FSC standards, which promote responsible management of forests around the world. Click on "Standards and Policies" to read their principles and criteria. The FSC logo (a combination of a checkmark and a tree) on wood and paper indicates certification.

- *Green Building A to Z: Understanding the Language of Green Building,* by Jerry Yudelson (Gabriola, B.C.: New Society Publishers, 2007). This book was written by an engineer who has trained thousands of people in the Leadership in Energy and Environmental Design (LEED) building rating system.

- *Green Building Products: The GreenSpec Guide to Residential Building Materials,* by Alex Wilson and Mark Piepkorn, revised 3rd edition (Brattleboro, Vt.: Building Green; Gabriola, B.C.: New Society Publishers, 2008). Though this book is written for residential projects, the information is pertinent to many church building and remodeling projects. The authors are associated with BuildingGreen.

- U.S. Green Building Council (USGBC), *www.usgbc.org*. The USGBC is a nonprofit organization that promotes green building practices and certifies sustainable buildings through their LEED four-level green building rating system. The website provides many links to relevant resources.

CONDUCT AN ENERGY AUDIT

Facts

- The essential first step in reducing energy use is to assess the amount, type, and patterns of energy use in your building, and to determine where energy is being wasted.

- Energy audits can be done in-house by knowledgeable members of the congregation using do-it-yourself energy audit instructions, or by paid professionals. Local electric and gas companies are also likely either to provide the service or to help guide you through the process.

- Making changes to address energy inefficiency and waste as identified by an energy audit reduces energy use, financial costs, and environmental costs (pollution and global warming).

- Saving energy makes good business sense.

Actions

◆ *Research your options* for having an energy audit.

◆ Complete the *energy audit.*

◆ *Implement the recommended changes* beginning with the no-cost and low-cost ones and moving on to the larger changes as your finances and circumstances allow.

Resources

◆ Database of State Incentives for Renewables and Efficiency (DSIRE), *www.dsireusa.org.* This is a project of the Solar Center, College of Engineering at North Carolina State University, and the Interstate Renewable Energy Council funded by the U.S. Department of Energy. The website is a state-by-state source of federal, state, local, and utility incentives and rebates that promote renewable energy and energy efficiency.

◆ The Regeneration Project and the Interfaith Power and Light (IPL) campaign, 220 Montgomery Street, suite 450, San Francisco, CA 94104; (415) 561-4891; *www.theregenerationproject.org.* This interfaith ministry focuses on the connection between ecology and faith. Through the IPL campaign congregations around the country are "mobilizing a national religious response to global warming." The website provides links to state-by-state Interfaith Power and Light programs and an online energy efficiency store for faith communities, *www.shopIPL.org.* It also offers a video, *Lighten Up! A Religious Response to Global Warming.*

◆ U.S. Department of Energy, Energy Efficiency and Renewable Energy, *www.eere.energy.gov/consumer/your_workplace.* Click on "Religious Institutions." This government website provides information and resources about energy audits; designing, remodeling, or construction of a building; appliances; electronic and office equipment; lighting; heating and cooling; water heaters; windows, doors, and skylights; buying clean electricity; and using renewable energy.

REDUCE ENERGY USE

Facts

* Emission of carbon dioxide (CO_2) and other greenhouse gases (GHGs) produces global warming.*

* GHGs other than CO_2 include methane, nitrous oxide, sulfur hexafluoride, chlorofluorocarbons, and others.

* Burning of fossil fuels (oil, coal, natural gas) for electricity and transportation produces carbon emissions.

* Americans use way too much fossil fuel energy.

* The average person in the United States generates five times the carbon emissions of the average person in China, and two hundred times that of a person in the poorest countries (Marland, Boden, and Andres 2007).

* Scientists worldwide report that rapidly escalating climate change is being caused mainly by human activities rather than by naturally occurring fluctuations, and they project dire consequences as a result (see the Ecology section of the Appendix).

---

*Carbon emissions are frequently reported instead of CO_2 emissions. According to T. J. Blasing at CDIAC (Carbon Dioxide Information Analysis Center (personal communication, June 4, 2008), CO_2 emissions include the *carbon and the oxygen;* carbon emissions include *only the carbon* contained in the CO_2. Because the molecular weight of carbon is 12, and O2 has a molecular weight of 16 x 2 = 32, the molecular weight of CO_2 is 12 + 32 = 44. CO_2 is thus $^{44}/_{12}$ heavier than carbon alone. To convert from carbon to carbon dioxide, multiply by $^{44}/_{12}$, or 3.667.

- Though the Earth is already experiencing many negative consequences of global warming, it is not too late to take actions to significantly reduce our energy use and its consequences.

- Individuals and nations around the world have recently awakened to the seriousness of the problems, and have begun tightening their energy belts.

- Churches have a responsibility to do this too.

- Changes we make that reduce energy consumption in our churches *do* make a difference.

Actions

- *Implement your energy audit recommendations* as fully as possible.

- *Join* the EPA's "Energy Star for Congregations" program and use their helpful resources.

- *Cut energy use* every way possible:

  > Turn off lights when they are not in use.

  > Use compact florescent light bulbs.

  > Turn down the heat.

  > Turn the air-conditioning off or to a higher temperature.

  > Purchase "Energy Star" appliances, electronics, lighting, and other products.

  > Insulate the building.

  > Plant shade trees.

  > Position windows for fair-weather breezes.

  > Turn off computers, printers, copiers, and televisions when they are not in use.

> Connect electronic equipment to power strips. Turn off the power strips when the equipment is not in use and overnight (because electronic equipment draws "phantom load" power even when turned off).

> Unplug cell phone chargers when not in use because they can also draw phantom load power.

> Car pool.

> Walk, ride a bicycle, or take public transportation.

> Consolidate errands and driving trips.

> Eliminate unnecessary driving and flying trips.

◆ Contact your denomination for information on their environmental stewardship programs. See the contact information in the websites section beginning on page 129.

Resources

◆ Carbon Dioxide Information Analysis Center (CDIAC), Oak Ridge National Laboratory, U.S. Department of Energy, Oak Ridge, Tennessee. This is the primary climate change data and information analysis center for the U.S. Department of Energy. For statistics related to carbon emissions by country, click on *cdiac.ornl.gov/trends/emis/tre_coun.html.*

◆ Climate.org, 1785 Massachusetts Ave. NW, Washington DC 20036; (202) 547-0104; *www.climate.org/climate_main.shtml.* This project of the Climate Institute provides information on climate change, energy, and the environment.

◆ Earth Policy Institute, 1350 Connecticut Ave. NW, Washington DC 20036; (202) 496-9290; *www.earth-policy.org.* Click on "Eco-Economy Indicators" for text and charts of worldwide population, carbon emission, and other trends.

- Energy Star, *www.energystar.gov/index.cfm?c=about.ab_ index*. This is a joint program of the U.S. Environmental Protection Agency and the U.S. Department of Energy. Their "Energy Star for Congregations" program at *www.energystar.gov/congregations* provides information for faith organizations about saving energy and money through the use of "efficient equipment, facility upgrades and maintenance." A wealth of free information and assistance is available to congregations, including a how-to guide (*Putting Energy into Stewardship: Congregations Guide*) and technical resources as well as technical assistance by email, public relations materials, and planning strategies.

- Green America (formerly Co-op America), 1612 K St. NW, Suite 600, Washington, DC 20006; (800) 584-7336; *www.greenamericatoday.org/programs/climate*. This not-for-profit membership organization focuses on using economic power to create a socially just and sustainable society. It provides online and print publications, education/information, and action campaigns. (After twenty-five years, Co-op America changed its name to Green America, effective January 1, 2009.)

- National Council of Churches Eco-Justice Programs, 110 Maryland Ave. NE, Suite 108, Washington, DC 20002; (202) 544-2350; *nccecojustice.org./about.html*. This program of the National Council of Churches of Christ provides information, education, an "Activist's Toolbox" of environmental stewardship actions, links to multiple faith-based environmental resources, and online downloadable resources.

- The National Religious Partnership for the Environment, 49 S. Pleasant St., Suite 301, Amherst, MA 01002; (413) 253-1515; *www.nrpe.org*. This partnership between the U.S. Conference of Catholic Bishops, the National Council of Churches of Christ, the Coalition on Environment and Jewish Life, and the Evangelical Environmental Network provides resources for "people of faith to weave values and programs of care for God's creation throughout the entire fabric of religious life." The website provides information on many environmental issues from various religious perspectives.

- The Regeneration Project and the Interfaith Power and Light (IPL) campaign, 220 Montgomery Street suite 450, San Francisco, CA 94104; (415) 561-4891; *www.theregenerationproject.org*. This interfaith ministry is focused on the connection between ecology and faith. Through the IPL campaign, congregations around the country are "mobilizing a national religious response to global warming." The website provides state-by-state information, links to related resources, and an online energy efficiency store for faith communities, *www.shopIPL.org*. It also offers a video, *Lighten Up! A Religious Response to Global Warming*.

CHANGE LIGHT BULBS

Facts

- Lights use electricity; most electricity is produced by burning fossil fuels.

- Burning fossil fuels produces carbon emissions.

- Carbon emissions contribute to global warming.

- *Energy Star* is a joint program of the U.S. Environmental Protection Agency and the U.S. Department of Energy to aid consumers in saving money and protecting the environment.

- Energy Star–qualified compact fluorescent lamps (CFLs) use up to 75 percent less energy than incandescent bulbs.

+ CFLs:

  > last up to ten times longer than incandescent bulbs

  > generate approximately 75 percent less heat than incandescent bulbs

  > can be used in regular light bulb sockets

  > are available for indoor and outdoor use in a range of wattages and styles including decorative, floodlight, and dimmable versions

  > produce varying shades of white light, which are measured in Kelvin units (K); warm white light, similar to incandescent light, is in the 2700–3000K range

  > save electricity — which translates into saving money

+ According to Energy Star, if every U.S. household replaced just one light bulb with an Energy Star qualified CFL, in one year we would prevent GHG emissions equivalent to the emissions of more than eight hundred thousand cars.

+ A small amount of mercury is sealed within a CFL. The average amount is about five milligrams. For comparison, older model thermometers contained about five hundred milligrams — so the mercury in a hundred CFLs is equal to the amount of mercury in one old thermometer or in one dental amalgam filling.

+ CFLs can be recycled in some localities. Contact your electric company for details about recycling and proper disposal.

+ Many governments have announced or proposed plans to phase out the sale of inefficient incandescent bulbs. Australia will have phased them out by 2010; Canada by 2012. The European Union countries are also on track to phase them out. The U.S. energy bill enacted in December 2007 will phase out incandescent bulbs in two stages, though over a long period of time (through 2020); in the meantime, individual states such as California and Nevada have taken action. Countries all over the world are working on phase-out plans (Asia-Pacific Economic Cooperation 2008).

- Light-emitting diodes (LEDs) are the small lights used in electronics. They can be used in Exit signs to reduce energy use and CO_2 pollution significantly. Annual energy use of an LED Exit sign that operates twenty-four hours a day = 44 kWh, compared to 140 kWh for fluorescent or CFL bulbs, and 350 kWh for incandescents. Annual CO_2 pollution for an LED Exit sign = 72 pounds, versus 230 pounds for fluorescents or CFLs, and 574 pounds for incandescents.

- LED lamps are starting to become available.

- Strings of lights for Christmas trees or other holiday decorating are now available in LEDs. They are cooler, safer, and very energy efficient.

- Solar-powered strings of lights are also available.

Actions

- *Replace incandescent light bulbs* with compact fluorescents.

- *Turn off lights* that are not in use.

- *Use lower lighting* when appropriate.

- *Use fewer lights* when possible.

- *Sell CFLs* as a fundraising and educational project.

- *Use light-emitting diodes* (LEDs) in Exit signs that run continuously.

- *Watch for new low energy lighting options* as technology continues to improve.

Resources

- Energy Star light bulb information is available at *www
  .energystar.gov* under "Lighting." A chart shows the light
  output equivalency between incandescent bulbs and CFLs, and
  state-by-state disposal information is detailed at *www.epa.gov/
  bulbrecycling*. The Energy Star website is the source of the
  CFL and LED statistics quoted in the Facts section.

- Environmental Defense Fund, 257 Park Ave. South, New
  York, NY 10010; (800) 684-3322; *www2.edf.org/home.cfm*.
  Click on "Light Bulb Guide" for an easy-to-use worksheet.
  Enter the location, shape, features, and brightness needs for
  lights, and a list of bulbs that fit your criteria is displayed.

- National Council of Churches of Christ Eco-Justice Programs
  provides an "Energy Stewardship Guide for Congregations,"
  which includes a section on lighting, at *www.nccecojustice.org/
  energyguide.htm*.

BECOME CARBON NEUTRAL

Facts

- Being "carbon neutral" means counterbalancing the effects
  of carbon emissions caused by our personal, household, and
  business activities.

- After reducing energy use as much as possible, individuals,
  businesses, places of worship, and others can invest in
  companies that are building renewable energy projects to
  displace electricity produced by burning carbon-emitting fossil
  fuels. This is known as buying carbon offsets.

- Offsets fund projects that prevent carbon emissions roughly
  equal to the emissions your actions have caused.

- Electricity can be produced from renewable sources such as
  the sun, wind, and waves.

- Methane capture facilities convert methane to energy. (Methane is a greenhouse gas, though it receives less publicity than CO_2. Livestock and landfills produce it.)

- Purchasing "carbon offsets" is a way to invest in clean energy companies and support their renewable energy projects.

- Purchasing offsets is *not* a substitute for reducing energy use, which is the crucial first step.

- Purchasing offsets is a growing trend (Co-op America 2007).

- The 217th General Assembly (2006) of the Presbyterian Church (USA) offset 84.3 tons of carbon emissions from the conference and called on Presbyterians to live a carbon neutral life.

- Many others have made commitments to buying offsets and/or being carbon neutral (e.g., major sporting events like the Super Bowl, the Pro Bowl, and World Cup Soccer; major banks like Wells Fargo and the World Bank; cities like Vail, Colorado; large and small businesses, rock stars on tour, and brides and grooms for their weddings).

- If *they* can do it, so can we!

Actions

- *Calculate carbon emissions* for your church energy use, or for a specific event or trip (see "Carbon Calculators" in the Resources section below).

- *Purchase offsets* for some or all of your energy use from providers who are developing clean renewable energy (such as wind turbines and solar power). These are true offsets that displace electricity generated by burning fossil fuels (see "Carbon Offset Providers" in the Resources section below).

* *Evaluate the quality* of the carbon offset vendor and purchase from ones whose projects:
  > are specific
  > would not occur without outside investments through offsets
  > have a clear timeframe for happening
  > have been audited by an outside source to help ensure that the vendors are providing a good quality offset

* Purchase from providers who are *currently generating clean renewable energy* or whose projects reduce greenhouse gas emissions in other ways.

Resources

* Green America, 1612 K St. NW, Suite 600, Washington, DC 20006; (800) 584-7336; *www.greenamericatoday.org/ programs/climate.* This not-for-profit membership organization focuses on using economic power to create a socially just and sustainable society. It provides online and print publications, as well as education, information, and action suggestions about energy issues and offset programs. Green America is an invaluable resource.

* *Carbon Calculators:*
  > The Climate Trust: *www.carboncounter.org/offset-your-emissions/personal-calculator.aspx*
  > U.S. Environmental Protection Agency: *www.epa.gov/ climatechange/emissions/ind_calculator.html*
  > *Native*Energy: *www.nativeenergy.com/pages/individuals/ 3.php*
  > Sustainable Travel International: *www.newdream.org/ consumer/myclimate.html*
  > TerraPass: *www.terrapass.com*

◆ *Carbon Offset Providers:*

> *Native*Energy, (800) 924-6826; *www.nativeenergy.com.* In addition to its other calculators, this website provides a tool specifically for organizations to calculate the emissions related to a conference or other event.

> TerraPass, (877) 879-8026; *www.terrapass.com.* Provides calculators for estimating emissions generated by driving and flying, by your home and business, and even emissions related to a wedding. This company also offers a "dorm offset" for college students.

> The Climate Trust, (503) 238-1915; *www.climatetrust.org/about_offsets.php.* Provides home, business, auto and air travel, and event calculators. This company also enables businesses to set up an employee offset program with a company-branded web page where employees can go to offset their carbon emissions; their company can then match the employees' contributions. A church could choose to establish this program for its members.

> Also see: New American Dream; *www.newdream.org/consumer/carbon.php* for links to auto-related, residential, and travel offsets.

REDUCE PAPER USE

Facts

◆ Producing paper requires a tremendous amount of natural resources — trees, water, and energy.

◆ It creates air and water pollution and contributes to global warming.

◆ The average office worker uses ten thousand sheets of copy paper each year.

- Over 40 percent of wood pulp goes toward the production of paper.

- About 40 percent of all municipal solid waste in the United States is paper.

- A forest area the size of twenty football fields is lost every minute to paper production.

- Industrialized nations have 20 percent of the world's population and consume 87 percent of the world's printing and writing papers.

- Producing one ton of paper requires two to three times that weight in trees.

- It takes more than one and a half cups of water to make one sheet of paper.

- Not all recycled paper is created equal. The higher the post-consumer recycled content, the fewer natural resources required.

- Using forty cases of *30 percent post-consumer recycled* content paper instead of virgin pulp paper saves the equivalent of:

  > 7.2 trees (40′ tall, 6–8″ in diameter)

  > 2,100 gallons of water

  > 1,230 kWh of electricity

  > 18 pounds of air pollution

- Using forty cases of *100 percent post-consumer recycled* content paper saves the equivalent of:

  > 24 trees

  > 7,000 gallons of water

> 4,100 kWh of electricity

> 60 pounds of air pollution

♦ Reducing paper use reduces greenhouse gases.

— Statistics gathered from Conservatree, Green America, and
Minnesota Pollution Control Agency. See the Resources section below.

Actions

♦ *Think before you print,* and print only what you need.

♦ *Think before you copy,* and copy only when necessary.

♦ *Use both sides* of all paper.

♦ *Use the blank sides* of paper that comes into the office printed on one side only.

♦ *Communicate electronically* when possible.

♦ *Buy only paper with recycled content.* The higher the recycled content the better.

♦ *Buy 100 percent recycled* paper when possible and appropriate for the use.

♦ Buy paper with the *highest post-consumer recycled content* you can find.

♦ *Consider using tree-free,* eco-paper made from agricultural residue fibers, textile residue, and plants such as bamboo, jute, flax, hemp, and kenaf. Search "tree-free paper" on the Internet for sources.

♦ *Post* an information sheet or agenda instead of making a copy for each person.

♦ *Eliminate* fax cover sheets.

♦ *Stop junk mail* by calling companies to be taken off their mailing lists, and/or by creating an easy-to-use form letter for this purpose. Contact the Direct Marketing Association listed in Resources for details.

+ *Reuse envelopes.*

+ *Recycle* paper.

Resources

+ Conservatree, 100 Second Ave., San Francisco, CA 94118; (415) 561-6530; *www.conservatree.org.* This is a comprehensive source of information about paper production, use, and selection, and it provides easy-to-use information as well as links for purchasing recycled paper.

+ Direct Marketing Association, 1120 Ave. of the Americas, New York, NY 10036-6700; (212) 768-7277; *www.dmaconsumers .org/cgi/offmailing.* Use this site for online and mail methods to register for Mail Preference Service (MPS) to decrease unsolicited mail including advertisements, catalogs, and credit card offers. (MPS applies to home addresses.)

+ Environmental Defense Fund, 257 Park Ave. South, New York, NY 10010; (800) 684-3322; *www2.edf.org/home.cfm.* Use their "Paper Calculator" at *www.papercalculator.org* to compare the use of large quantities of different types of papers with different recycled content to determine the differences in the amount of wood and energy used, and the amount of greenhouse gases, waste water, and solid waste generated. This information can be used to inform paper purchasing decisions.

+ Environmental Paper Network; *www.environmentalpaper.org.* This website provides a guide for paper purchasers, paper use statistics, education materials, and related links. Click on "Tools & Resources."

+ Green America, 1612 K St. NW, Suite 600, Washington DC 20006; (800) 584-7336; *www.greenamericatoday.org.*

Click on "Programs," then "Woodwise." Also see the Green America *National Green Pages* for sources of recycled and tree-free paper.

◆ Minnesota Pollution Control Agency: *http://reduce.org*. Click on "Office Paper" and "At the Office." This website offers a wealth of information, downloadable fact sheets and posters, a "paper-less toolkit," and related links.

RECYCLE
(ALUMINUM, GLASS, STEEL CONTAINERS)

Facts

◆ Recycling preserves natural resources and reduces pollution.

◆ The keys to decreasing waste are **Rethink, Reduce, Reuse, Recycle.** *Note:* Recycle is at the end of the list—*after* we have done the first three.

◆ *Rethinking* our "needs" and practices, *reducing* what we "need" and what we buy, and *reusing* what we or others already have are the first steps.

◆ According to the U.S. EPA, in 2006 recycling diverted 82 million tons of material from landfills and incinerators. Approximately nine thousand curbside recycling programs exist and serve about half of our population. However, we still recycle less than one-third of our waste. This is what *is* recycled:

  > 25 percent of glass containers

  > 52 percent of paper

  > 45–50 percent of aluminum beverage cans

  > 63 percent of steel containers

  > 67 percent of major appliances

- Glass containers are 100 percent recyclable. Every ton of glass recycled saves a ton of raw materials.

- Aluminum beverage cans are 100 percent recyclable. According to Earth911.com, throwing away an aluminum can is equivalent to wasting half of the can's volume in gasoline.

- Steel cans contain from 25 percent to 100 percent recycled steel.

- Less than one-third of plastic soft drink bottles and one-fourth of plastic water bottles are recovered and downcycled (see "Avoid Plastic-Bottled Water" in the "Products" chapter, page 58).

Actions

- *Rethink* current purchasing and use practices.

- *Eliminate or reduce* use wherever possible.

- *Buy glass, steel, or aluminum* containers instead of plastic when possible.

- *Write letters* to manufacturers encouraging them to package their products in truly recyclable containers.

- *Avoid* buying water bottled in plastic containers.

- *Contact* your local government or private recycling projects to find out what and how to recycle in your area.

- *Become involved* in starting recycling (or support others' efforts) if it does not already exist locally.

- *Provide receptacles* for recycling at your church that are clearly marked and easily accessible.

- *Recycle* all glass, steel, and aluminum containers.

Resources

◆ Container Recycling Institute, *www.container-recycling.org*. This website has a continually updated total of the number of beverage containers that have been "landfilled, littered and incinerated in the U.S. so far this year"; when I accessed it on May 31, 2008, it was over 53 *billion* so far in 2008. Check out today's numbers.

◆ Earth911.com, 14646 N. Kierland Blvd., Suite 100, Scottsdale, AZ 85254; (480) 889-2650; *earth911.com*. This site tells why and what to recycle, and provides a step-by-step list of how to get started and a guide to starting an office recycling program.

◆ The National Recycling Coalition, at *www.nrc-recycle.org/ americarecycles,* is a national nonprofit organization that promotes "recycling, waste prevention, composting, and reuse" and sponsors America Recycles Day each year on November 15.

◆ U.S. Environmental Protection Agency, Ariel Rios Building, 1200 Pennsylvania Ave. NW, Washington, DC 20460; *www.epa.gov/osw.* This is the EPA site related to "Wastes." Click on "Recycling/Pollution Prevention" for information on climate change, reduce/reuse/recycle, closing the loop by buying recycled products, and other related topics.

HANDLE E-WASTE RESPONSIBLY

Facts

◆ Old computers, TVs, video and DVD players, stereos, MP3 players, and cell phones become electronic waste or "e-waste."

◆ e-waste = hazardous waste.

◆ e-waste contains lead, chromium, cadmium, mercury, beryllium, nickel, zinc, and brominated flame retardants.

- In 2005, 1.5–1.9 million tons of e-waste went to landfills (EPA 2008b).

- Each day in the United States, 100,000 computers become obsolete (Tarver-Wahlquist 2007).

- The Basel Convention on the Control of Transboundary Movements of Hazardous Wastes and Their Disposal was adopted in Basel, Switzerland, in 1989 and went into force in 1992. It was strengthened by the Basel Ban, which banned (effective January 1, 1998) all forms of hazardous waste exports from the wealthiest most industrialized countries to developing countries.

- Countries that have ratified the Basel Ban must take responsibility for recycling their own e-waste instead of shipping it to poor regions of the world where workers are subjected to toxic working conditions for little pay.

- France, Germany, Italy, Spain, and the United Kingdom have all ratified the Basel Conventions's Ban.

- The United States has *not* ratified the Basel Convention's Ban.

- The Basel Action Network (BAN) is an organization focused on banning toxic waste dumping on the world's poorest countries.

- According to BAN, 50–80 percent of e-waste delivered to recyclers is shipped to Asia and Africa, where it is either dumped or improperly processed at the expense of poor people.

- Electronic products are made from valuable resources.

- e-waste events that take old electronic equipment for free are not necessarily recycling it responsibly. (See the Federal Electronics Challenge website and the EPA website in Resources for more information).

◆ Reusing and recycling the materials saves natural resources and generates less pollution than does the manufacturing of totally new electronic products.

◆ The European Union countries, Australia, Canada, Japan, New Zealand, and others have some form of extended producer responsibility (EPR) laws that hold manufacturers financially responsible for the post-consumer stage of their products. The United States does not (Imhoff 2005).

◆ In 2005 California enacted a fee on electronic products to be paid by the consumer at purchase and used to pay for recycling services.

◆ In 2006 Maine enacted the first state law requiring manufacturers to pay for the recycling of their discarded e-waste.

◆ Reliable information is available about what to do with e-waste (See Resources).

Actions

◆ *Ask questions* prior to purchase, and look for electronic products that:

> contain fewer toxins. (See the Electronic Product Environmental Assessment Tool in the Resources section below for further information.)

> use recycled materials

> are labeled "Energy Star"

> are well designed for easy upgrading and recycling

> use minimal packaging

> are made by companies that have take-back programs

◆ Have equipment *repaired or upgraded* to extend its life.

◆ *Donate* used but still usable electronic products to charities, schools, or others.

◆ *Use manufacturers' take-back programs.*

◆ *Recycle* with a service that has taken the *BAN pledge* to assure that they do not send e-waste to landfills, incinerators, or to prisons or developing countries for recycling. Find the pledge and recyclers who have signed at *www.ban.org/pledge1.html.*

◆ *Write letters* to manufacturers encouraging them to design environmentally responsible electronics and to implement take-back programs.

◆ *Support* extended producer responsibility (EPR) legislation.

◆ Use your *purchasing power voice.* Buy as green as possible.

Resources

◆ Basel Action Network, c/o Earth Economics, 122 S. Jackson, Suite 320, Seattle, WA 98104; (206) 652-5555; *www.ban.org.* This is an organization that works to confront the global toxic waste trade and address the resultant human rights, health, and environmental issues. Their "Basel Convention on the Control of Transboundary Movements of Hazardous Wastes and Their Disposal" was adopted in 1989 and went into effect in 1992. The website provides information about e-waste, the effects of the toxic waste trade, and the toxic trade ban status of countries. It also shows report cards on countries' ratification of four related international treaties. On the latter, Denmark, France, Germany, Spain, the U.K., and others ranked "excellent," many ranked anywhere from "very good" to "fair," and the United States along with Russia, Malta, and Israel, ranked "failing."

◆ Earth911.com; *http://earth911.com/electronics.* This section of the Earth911.com website provides information about the hazards of e-waste and how to handle it responsibly.

- Electronic Product Environmental Assessment Tool (EPEAT), *www.epeat.net*. EPEAT provides information about the environmental attributes of desktop computers, notebook computers, and monitors. These products are evaluated on twenty-three required criteria and twenty-eight optional criteria. Ones that meet all the required criteria are then ranked by a three-tiered system (bronze, silver, and gold). Click on the "Search Product Registry" box near the top left corner. This allows you to search a product by type of equipment and manufacturer. Then it ranks the product and provides detailed information about specific areas such as materials used, end of life design, longevity, corporate performance, and packaging. This website is informative and useful in making purchasing decisions.

- The Electronics TakeBack Coalition, (415) 206-9595; *www.computertakeback.com/about/index.cfm* is a campaign to get manufacturers to take responsibility for the life cycle of their electronic products through the creation of extended producer responsibility (EPR).

- Energy Star, *www.energystar.gov/index.cfm?c=home.index*. This program designates Energy Star status to products that meet EPA and Department of Energy guidelines for energy efficiency. Click on "Products," then "Office Equipment."

- Environmental Protection Agency (EPA), *www.epa.gov/epaoswer/hazwaste/recycle/ecycling*. This website provides a good source of information about related government programs, where to donate or recycle old electronics, and the specifics about manufacturers' take-back programs. Also of interest are statistics, publications, and the FAQs. Under "Frequent Questions," click on "Electronics Recycler Certification."

- The Federal Electronics Challenge program, online at *www.federalelectronicschallenge.net*, encourages federal facilities and agencies to adopt environmentally friendly practices in their purchase and use of electronic products. Click on "Resources," "End-of-life Management," then "Recycling" to access their "Checklist for the Selection of Electronic Recycling Services" and other informative documents.

- Green America, 1612 K St. NW, Suite 600, Washington DC 20006; (800) 584-7336; *greenamericatoday.org*. Type "e-waste" into "Search" for related articles found at various locations on the website. Click on "Publications," then "Green American" to access "The Perils of E-waste" article in the Fall 2007 issue.

- Green Disk, (800) 308-DISK, (425) 392-8700; online at *www.greendisk.com*. For a fee this company supplies packs and boxes for collecting "techotrash" so it can be sent to them for responsible recycling.

- Greenpeace, "Your Guide to Green Electronics," online at *www.greenpeace.org/international/news/green-electronics-guide-ewaste250806*. A report and an easy-to-read scorecard rank the major electronics firms as to their records on use of toxic chemicals and their recycling programs. The graphic scorecard ranks companies on a ten-point scale and shows multiple updates each year beginning in August 2006. This can inform your product purchase decisions.

- Maine Bureau of Remediation and Waste Management; *maine.gov/dep/rwm/ewaste/index.htm*. You can take a look at Maine's forward-looking e-waste law at this website.

Chapter Two

The Grounds

The area surrounding your church — whether vast or tiny; rural, suburban, or urban; elaborate or modest — reflects and projects the meaning, mission, and tenor of your house of worship. It is an outward expression of the inner workings of the church.

Even a small space can beautify a church and give silent voice to the congregation's respect for and love of God's creation. If you have room for one tree, one hedge, or one small planted area, you have room to honor the Earth. If you are fortunate enough to have a large area that can be planted and used to reflect your church's green values, so much the better. (Those with no space at all for plantings can honor the Earth in other ways as described throughout *Eco-Faith*.) Regardless of your congregation's size, funds, or skills, the church grounds are an integral part of an environmental stewardship mission.

This chapter focuses on multiple aspects of greening your church grounds: saving energy by strategic planting, saving water by choosing plants wisely, reducing or eliminating noise and air pollution by using the right equipment, and eliminating soil and water pollution by using only safe pest control and fertilizing methods. In addition this chapter offers suggestions for learning to turn your garden trimmings and kitchen scraps into a source of vital nutrients for your plants; I suggest that composting can be a practical, ecological, and spiritual action. I also suggest incorporating plants native to your region as a way to be part of a growing trend to help reestablish plants that have been nearly decimated due to building and infrastructure development and the introduction of non-native plant species. I recommend various theme gardens; these can enrich both the creators and users of the gardens. For example, a Bible garden, in which some of the 100+ plants mentioned in the Bible are featured, can be educational, an impetus for Bible study, a place for sharing work and thoughts, and a place for quiet reflection. Gardens that provide food are functional, but can also be used to further our understanding of the connection between food and faith, and the interrelationship of food, climate change, poverty, and hunger.

Any and all gardens nurture the souls of those who enter. The church grounds can be more than grass and a parking lot; they can be part of the sanctuary — part of the spiritual life of the church.

The chapter offers **Facts**, suggestions for **Actions**, and **Resources** on the topics of landscaping, using native plants, creating a Bible garden, and composting. Learn, be creative, and dig in.

LANDSCAPE GREEN

Facts

- Environmentally friendly landscaping:

  > saves money, energy, and water

  > attracts birds, butterflies, and beneficial insects

  > provides energy-saving shade and wind blocks

  > reduces or eliminates the need for toxic chemicals

  > reduces air, water, and noise pollution

  > is healthier for people and the planet

- Tens of millions of pounds of pesticides are used on lawns annually.

- Pesticides run off lawns and pollute rivers, lakes, and the ocean.

- Humans are exposed to toxic pesticides that are applied to landscapes.

- Alternatives to toxic pesticides exist — both products and practices.

- Mulch reduces weeds and improves water retention of soil.

- Compost is a soil amendment and fertilizer that can be made on site.

- Plant trimmings, grass clippings, and leaves can be shredded and composted instead of sent to the landfill.

- Up to 60 percent of total water use in some areas of the United States goes to maintain lawns.

- Wise landscaping greatly reduces water use.

- Parking lots, driveways, and sidewalks constructed with porous materials allow water to seep into the ground. This helps prevent storm water runoff, erosion, and flash flooding and filters out some of the vehicle-generated pollutants before they enter the groundwater or public waterways.

- Porous asphalt, permeable pavers, pervious concrete, and plantable pavers are storm water management options.

- Storm water can be captured and used or slowed and diverted to decrease runoff and to mitigate its pollution of surface water. Vegetated roofs and rain gardens are useful for this purpose.

- Not all landscape architects and lawn maintenance companies are knowledgeable about or committed to environmentally friendly landscaping practices, though some specialize in this area.

♦ Developing church gardens can be a shared and a unifying effort that combines the interests of many church members, raises environmental awareness, and promotes Earth-friendly landscaping practices not only at the church, but at members' homes.

Actions

♦ *Brainstorm* landscape and garden ideas with the congregation.

♦ *Consider creating themed areas.* Some possibilities are native plant, meditation, memorial, herb, vegetable, flower, Bible (see "Create a Bible Garden," page 51 below), or children's gardens.

♦ *Consult* a landscape architect or other garden planner.

♦ *Choose to work with someone who is knowledgeable* about environmentally friendly practices and whose landscaping values match those of the church.

♦ *Use some native plants* (see the "Use Native Plants" section, page 50 below).

♦ *Ask members to donate a plant* from their home garden to create a sense of belonging to the church.

♦ *Choose pest-resistant* plants.

♦ *Choose easy-to-maintain* plants.

♦ *Use hand tools and reel mowers* when possible instead of gas-powered equipment.

♦ *Do not use* noise- and air-polluting leaf blowers.

♦ Apply only *nontoxic, organic fertilizers and pesticides.*

♦ *Incorporate edible plants* into the garden plan.

- *Share vegetables* with the local food bank, homeless shelter, or other social service group.

- *Plant trees* for shade and wind block.

- *Use xeriscape* (low water use and drought-tolerant) plants.

- *Use the most efficient irrigation* and watering schedules.

- *Compost* organic materials (see the "Compost" section page 53 below).

- *Use Earth-friendly structural, decorative, and paving* (e.g., planted fences versus vinyl fencing; porous driveways and sidewalks versus impermeable surfaces that create runoff problems).

- Use no lighting, low-level lighting, or *solar lighting.*

- *Use signage* to identify garden areas and create interest in them.

- *Cut flowers* from the flower garden to decorate the sanctuary during services.

- *Make table centerpieces* from flowers, fruits, vegetables, and herbs.

- *Hold Sunday school classes and meetings* in the gardens.

- *Plant a tree as part of a dedication ceremony* for a landscape project or for other celebrations and memorials.

- *Connect with God* through nature.

- *Enjoy* your money-saving, functional, restorative, and beautiful natural spaces.

Resources

- GreenScapes, *www.epa.gov/greenscapes.* This program of the U.S. Environmental Protection Agency offers "cost-efficient and environmentally friendly solutions for landscaping." The website provides information and resources; online calculators to assist in decision making related to landscape design, construction, and maintenance; a "Tip Sheet" to help you reduce or eliminate the monetary and environmental costs of landscape-related actions; and links to other relevant websites.

◆ National Coalition for Pesticide-Free Lawns, 701 E St. SE, #200, Washington, DC 20003; (202) 543-5450; *www.beyondpesticides.org/pesticidefreelawns/index*. This website provides information, education, links to related resources, and a metal "Pesticide-Free Zone" sign for display on your lawn.

◆ Toolbase Services, *www.toolbase.org/index.aspx*. To locate information about storm water management, go to "Home Building Topics," "Green Building," and then click on "Low Impact Development Practices for Storm Water Management," "Permeable Pavement," and "Rainwater Harvesting."

◆ Union of Concerned Scientists, 2 Brattle Square, Cambridge, MA 02238; (617) 547-5552; *www.ucsusa.org/publications/greentips/0804-pest-control-without-risks*. "Greentips: Environmental Ideas in Action" provides brief articles about various topics including "Pest Control without Risks" about nontoxic pest control for the garden. Click on the Greentips archives "Choose a Topic" for other helpful articles.

◆ U.S. Environmental Protection Agency (EPA), Natural Landscaping Workgroup, 77 W. Jackson Boulevard (G-17J), Great Lakes National Program Office, Chicago, IL 60604; *www.epa.gov/greenacres*. This website provides information, PowerPoint presentations, fact sheets, slideshows, photos, and other resources about natural landscaping.

- *Xeriscape Handbook: A How-to Guide to Natural, Resource-Wise Gardening* by Gayle Weinstein (Golden, Colo.: Fulcrum, 1999). This book offers information about designing, choosing plants for, and maintaining a water-conserving landscape.

USE NATIVE PLANTS

Facts

- Native plants have evolved regionally over thousands of years and so are suited to specific geographical areas in terms of soil, sun and water needs, and pest resistance.

- Native plants are wonderful landscape plants.

- Native plants:

  > provide habitat for native birds, butterflies, and wildlife

  > are low maintenance

  > require no or little fertilizer or pesticides

  > are drought resistant

  > do not need to be mowed as do lawns, and so greatly reduce the need for air-polluting gasoline-using lawn maintenance tools

- Little-used lawn areas around the church can be converted to native plant gardens or ground cover.

- Most U.S. native ecosystems (forests, wetlands, prairies) are long gone — replaced by urban and suburban developments, industrial complexes, and agriculture. Using native plants is a small step in restoring plant diversity and our native plant heritage.

- Use of native plants is a growing trend.

Actions

- *Educate yourself about plants native to your region* through books, local publications, your local Cooperative Extension office, and university resources.

- *Incorporate some native plants* into the church landscaping.

- *Post attractive signs* to identify the plants.

Resources

- U.S. Department of Agriculture, Cooperative State Research, Education, and Extension Service, *www.csrees.usda.gov/ Extension*. The Cooperative Extension System is a nationwide educational network. Each U.S. state and territory has an office at its land-grant university as well as local and regional offices. An online map allows the user quick access to information about the nearest Cooperative Extension office and so to a wealth of gardening and landscaping information specific to the region.

- U.S. Environmental Protection Agency (EPA), Natural Landscaping Workgroup, 77 W. Jackson Boulevard (G-17J), Great Lakes National Program Office, Chicago, IL 60604; *www.epa.gov/greenacres*. Their "Landscaping with Native Plants Fact Sheet" provides information about the benefits of using native plants, and which plants attract song birds, hummingbirds, and butterflies. It also has downloadable fact sheets for some specific regions of the country.

- Search your local library and bookstores for native plant resource books specific to your region.

CREATE A BIBLE GARDEN

Facts

- More than 125 different plants and trees are mentioned in the Old and New Testaments.

◆ Beautiful, interesting, and educational Bible gardens can be created to feature some of these plants.

Actions

◆ *Plan and design* a Bible garden as part of the church landscape.

◆ *Label the plantings* by common name, scientific name, and Bible reference.

◆ Include the appropriate *Bible verse* or summarize the Bible reference.

◆ Involve both *children and adults* in the planting and study of the garden and the Bible verses.

Resources

◆ *Flowers of the Bible: And How to Grow Them,* by Allan Swenson (New York: Citadel, 2002).

◆ *Healing Plants of the Bible: History, Lore, and Meditations,* by Vincenzina Krymow (Cincinnati: St. Anthony Messenger Press, 2002).

◆ *Healing Plants of the Bible: Their Uses Then and Now,* by Tim Morrison (Baltimore: PublishAmerica, 2002).

◆ *Herbs of the Bible,* by Allan Swenson (New York: Citadel, 2003).

◆ *Planting a Bible Garden: A Good Book Practical Guide,* by F. Nigel Hepper (Grand Rapids, Mich.: Fleming H. Revell, 1997).

◆ *The Plants of the Bible: And How to Grow Them,* by Allan Swenson (New York: Citadel, 2000).

◆ *www.BiblicalGardens.org.* This website provides information about designing and planting a Bible garden, with lists of plants and their biblical references. It also has virtual tours of biblical and other gardens and links to resources.

COMPOST

Facts

- Most "waste" from the landscape is really not waste at all, but instead is the source of compost.

- Bacteria, fungi, worms, and insects feed on the organic material in a compost pile or bin and transform it into a gorgeous, rich, fertile soil amendment, and mulch.

- Compost improves soil structure, texture, and fertility.

- Organically maintained landscapes produce toxin-free compost.

- Compostable yard and kitchen "waste" takes up 25–35 percent of landfill space.

- Composting diverts "waste" from landfills and recycles it back into the Earth.

- Leaves and trimmings are not waste.

- Leaves and trimmings are a *resource*.

- Composting is the ultimate recycling experience.

- Building a compost pile on the church grounds is a doable project.

- Churches can compost plant trimmings, leaves, and kitchen scraps.

- Some disposable plates and cups (e.g., those made of sugar cane waste) can be composted in your compost pile.

- Shredding materials speeds up the composting process.

- Vermicomposting, or worm composting, is another way to turn kitchen and paper scraps into a fertile soil amendment called "vermicast" (the castings produced by special worms as they eat the scraps).

- Worm composting bins work well for smaller amounts of scraps and can be kept inside.

- Composting is especially well-suited to churches due to its rich symbolism of rebirth and renewal and its tangible evidence of caring for God's Earth.

Actions

- *Read about* various composting methods.

- *Determine your composting needs and goals* (e.g., produce fertile mulch, save landfill space, save money on soil amendments, reduce weeds, reduce synthetic chemical use, provide a place for disposal of food scraps, use as an educational tool).

- *Choose a method that suits your needs* with regard to materials to be composted, time commitment, and available space.

- *Coordinate your composting plans* with those who do the landscaping and kitchen work.

- *Buy or build* your compost bin or pile.

- *Make and use* compost.

- *Reflect* on the cycle of nature and our ties to the Earth.

Resources

- *Basic Composting: All the Skills and Tools You Need to Get Started,* edited by Erich Ebeling (Mechanicsburg, Pa.: Stackpole Books, 2003). The contributors to this easy-to-read, spiral-bound book provide information on compost bins and piles, equipment, ingredients, uses, worm composting, and making compost tea. The book includes helpful pictures.

- Compost Guide: A Complete Guide to Composting, *www.compostguide.com/index.* This online source explains the benefits of composting, how and what to compost, and how to use the finished product. It provides a list of compostable and noncompostable materials, as well as a chart on troubleshooting composting problems. Finally, the book also explains worm composting.

- *Compost: Rodale Organic Gardening Basics,* vol. 8, by the editors of Rodale Organic Gardening Magazine and Books (Emmaus, Pa.: Rodale, 2001). This is but one of the many wonderful Rodale organic gardening books.

- Wormwoman, *www.wormwoman.com.* The website of the late Mary Appelhof and Flowerfield Enterprises provides information and resources on all things related to vermicomposting.

Chapter Three

Products

Churches are consumers. Food, beverages, plates, utensils, cleaning supplies, office paper and equipment, and more are purchased on a regular basis. To bring purchasing practices in line with our social, economic, and environmental values, we can take several important steps including buying fair trade, organic, and natural products.

Purchasing fair trade products is one way to promote social justice, address poverty issues, and ensure environmental stewardship in the production of the products. "Fair trade" refers to the development of direct trading partnerships that provide farmers, artisans, and other producers a fair wage so they can profitably maintain their small businesses. In addition to fair wages, the focus is on showing respect for the cultural values and identities of the producer communities and supporting sustainable local businesses that provide safe conditions for workers; do not use forced child labor; invest premiums paid for products into local educational, environmental, and other community development projects; and use environmentally friendly business practices (Mertz and Korfhage, n.d.; Fair Trade Federation 2008).

Fair trade means that money reaches the hands of the small farmer, seamstress, or artisan instead of going to high-commission middlemen/women. It is the *opposite* of the all-too-common economic practice of using the cheapest labor possible in terrible working conditions to mass produce products by using methods that pollute and degrade the natural environment and often destroy the social and cultural community of the workers. Instead of having to research companies to determine if they are involved in child or slave labor, sweat shops, or practices that pollute the air and water or destroy rainforests, we can buy Fair Trade Certified products and purchase from producers, wholesalers, or retailers who are members of the Fair Trade Federation. Then the work of researching the businesses' practices is done for us. We promote social justice, economic justice, and environmental justice just by choosing products wisely. Fair trade products do tend to cost a bit more, but when we factor in the "true cost" of cheaper goods — produced at the expense of workers' economic and physical health and at the expense of the health of the planet — fair trade items are a bargain. Buying fair trade products is a natural fit for people of faith simply because fair trade values are compatible with Christian values.

Other ways to wield purchasing power to engender positive and far-reaching social, economic, and environmental effects include buying organically grown food and fabrics, and buying locally grown and locally made products. In addition, we can choose to buy such items as paper products for the kitchen, bathroom, and office with a high recycled paper content; tree-free paper and flooring; and sustainably grown and harvested wood products. We can buy or make natural and nonpolluting cleaning supplies, and we can opt for compostable dinnerware when reusable is not an option. Most important, we can reduce what we purchase by rethinking our needs, reusing what we already have, and deciding *not* to buy certain Earth-*unfriendly* products — like polystyrene foam plates and cups, disposable dinnerware, and of course those ubiquitous plastic water bottles.

A word of caution as you choose your products: Read "Avoid Greenwashing" (page 76 below) to heighten your awareness of tricks of the consumer marketing trade and to increase your green consumer savvy.

The Products chapter offers **Facts**, suggestions for **Actions**, and a list of **Resources** for each action to help raise awareness in your congregation about the power of your purchasing dollar and the far-reaching social, economic, and environmental effects of your consumer choices.

AVOID PLASTIC-BOTTLED WATER

Facts

Water bottled in plastic is:

- bad for the environment

- a waste of money

- no better, and possibly worse, for our health than tap water

- a social justice issue

Environment

> According to the American Chemistry Council, less than 24 percent of plastic bottles were recycled in 2006.

> This means seven or eight of every ten bottles ends up in a landfill.

> *Tens of billions* of plastic water bottles are used in the United States each year.

> Plastic bottles are a petrochemical product, and millions of gallons of oil are used each year to make these bottles.

> Energy is consumed not only in the manufacture of plastic bottles, but also in their transport and disposal.

> *Plastic is not truly recyclable* and is not biodegradable. The breakdown of plastic can take thousands of years, and the components can seep into our water supplies.

> Plastic can sometimes be "down-cycled" into other products. It can usually be down-cycled *only one time* — then it is headed to the landfill.

Cost

> Bottled water costs the consumer four thousand to ten thousand times more than tap water.

> We spend about $11 billion each year on bottled water in the United States.

> Advertising has convinced people that we need to consume bottled water. Social norms (i.e., everyone is doing it) have further cemented this idea.

> 25 percent or more of bottled water is, yes, tap water.

Health Concerns

> A Natural Resources Defense Council study found contamination in excess of allowable limits in at least one sample of about one-third of the 103 brands of bottled water they tested.

> The EPA regulates the quality of tap water. The Food and Drug Administration regulates bottled water that crosses state lines. The EPA tap water regulations are more stringent than the FDA bottled water regulations.

Social Justice

> *One billion people around the world do not have safe drinking water.*

> Multinational corporations are privatizing springs and aquifers around the world and bottling water from them at the expense of rural household wells, wetlands, the depleted aquifers, and the people who depend on these water sources.

Trends

> Some U.S. cities are prohibiting the purchase of bottled water with city money.

> Some restaurants are no longer offering bottled water.

> The public is becoming increasingly aware of the enormous detrimental social and environmental costs of plastic bottled water.

— Statistics gathered from sources listed in Resources

Actions

◆ *Research the quality of your tap water* through your local water utility.

◆ *Educate your congregation* about water issues and plastic through bulletin inserts, newsletter and website articles, church practices, and/or sermons.

◆ *Drink tap water.*

◆ *Install a water filter* for drinking water if necessary.

◆ *Help establish new societal norms:*

> Carry your own individual *reusable water containers.*

> *Serve water from pitchers* or large thermal jugs at church social functions and meetings.

Resources

◆ Environmental Protection Agency, *www.epa.gov/safewater/dwh/index.* At "Ground Water and Drinking Water" click on "Drinking Water and Health Basics," and FAQs. A downloadable brochure, "Bottled Water Basics" provides definitions of terms and information on water standards and filtering.

◆ Food and Water Watch, 1616 P St. NW, Suite 300, Washington, DC 20036; (202) 683-2500; *www.foodandwaterwatch.org*. This nonprofit agency focuses on food and water safety for consumers.

◆ Natural Resource Defense Council, *www.nrdc.org*. Click on "Water," then "In Brief: Drinking Water," then "Bottled Water: FAQ" for related information. A "Consumer Guide to Water Filters" can be found at *www.nrdc.org/water/ drinking/gfilters.asp*. Check this for guidance in buying and maintaining a tap water filter. Go to *www.nrdc.org/ water/drinking/bw/bwinx.asp* to read the 1999 report on their four-year study of bottled water.

◆ Sierra Club, Water Privatization Task Force; *www.sierraclub .org/committees/cac/water*. This is an education and advocacy group of the Sierra Club that works to prevent corporate privatization of water and to greatly reduce the use of bottled water. The website provides information, articles, a PowerPoint presentation, and a downloadable brochure ("Bottled Water: Learning the Facts and Taking Action.")

CLEAN GREEN

Facts

◆ Many cleaning products contain toxic chemicals including formaldehyde, phenol, ammonia, ethanol, butane, and others.

◆ Chemicals can result in irritations of the skin, eye, nose, and throat, as well as dizziness and headaches. Fumes and fragrances may produce allergic reactions, and ingestion can cause stomach problems and even death. Lye-containing drain and oven cleaners can result in burns. Chlorine bleach can irritate the eyes, nose, throat, and lungs.

◆ Alkylphenol ethoxylates (APEs) are used in many cleaning products and can break down into nonylphenol, which can disrupt hormone functions in animals and possibly in humans.

◆ Prolonged chemical exposure might eventually lead to chemical sensitivities.

◆ Many cleaning products contain ingredients derived from petroleum, which is a nonrenewable resource. These products do not biodegrade easily, and so they end up and remain for extended periods in waterways, air, and soil where they negatively affect fish and other wildlife.

◆ When thrown in the trash, cleaning products can contaminate landfills.

◆ Phosphates in cleaning products are relatively safe for the user, but detrimental to the environment. They negatively affect water quality by causing rapid growth of algae, which use the oxygen in the water; fish and water insects then cannot survive.

◆ Antibacterial cleaning products possibly contribute to bacteria becoming antibiotic-resistant and thereby decrease the effectiveness of antibiotics for treating illnesses.

◆ Some products labeled "natural" contain toxic chemical ingredients.

◆ Approximately eighty thousand industrial chemicals are registered for use in the United States, but less than 20 percent have been tested to evaluate their effect on human and planetary health.

> —Information gathered from CHEC, Green America, INFORM, and the Union of Concerned Scientists. See the Resources section.

Actions

◆ *Read labels* and avoid those that say "Caution," "Warning," or "Danger."

◆ *Avoid* products that do not list the ingredients.

- *Avoid* products containing phosphates or EDTA (a phosphate substitute that degrades slowly).

- *Make nontoxic cleaning products* from natural ingredients like baking soda, borax, salt, white vinegar, lemon juice, vegetable oil-based soaps, olive oil, isopropyl alcohol, club soda, and essential oils.

- If purchasing cleaners, buy ones that are *concentrated,* and *buy in bulk* to reduce packaging waste.

- *Buy and use commercially produced "green" cleaning products.* Read labels and choose ones that provide specific information, not those with general or vague terms such as "natural."

- Look for *recycled, recyclable, and refillable containers* and packaging.

- *Use microfiber cloths and water* instead of paper towels and toxic cleaners to clean many surfaces.

Resources

- Biokleen, P.O. Box 820689, Vancouver, WA 98682; (800) 477-0188; *www.biokleenhome.com.* Established in 1989, this company develops and sells products based on their standards, which require that they be effective, concentrated, nontoxic, and environmentally safe. Products are sold in both household and commercial sizes.

- Children's Health Environmental Coalition (CHEC), 12300 Wilshire Blvd., Suite 320, Los Angeles, CA 90025; (310) 820-2030; *www.checnet.org/about_main.asp.* This is a national nonprofit organization that provides education about environmental toxins, especially as related to children's health.

- Citra-Solv, LLC, P.O. Box 2597, Danbury, CT 06813-2597; (203) 778-0881; *www.citra-solv.com/index.html.* This company develops and sells a large variety of cleaners made from renewable resources with the aim of offering products that work well yet result in minimum environmental impact. Products are developed with no animal testing.

- *Clean Your Home Healthy: Green Cleaning Made Easy* by Candita Clayton with Bryna Rene (Garden City, N.Y.: Morgan James Publishing, 2008). Some of the environmentally friendly home cleaning tips in this book can be adapted for church use.

- Earth Friendly Products, 44 Green Bay Rd., Winnetka, IL 60093; (800) 335-3267; *www.ecos.com/shop.html*. A maker of all natural, plant-based products, which are all made in their U.S. factories.

- EcoMall, *www.ecomall.com/homepage.htm*. This online store is a source for ecological information, articles, and cleaning (and other) product information.

- Ecover Inc., 2760 E. Spring St., Suite 220, Long Beach, CA 90806; (800) 449-4925; *www.ecover.com/us/en*. Established in 1980 in Belgium, this international company makes green products for home and commercial use that are marketed in more than twenty countries.

- Green America, 1612 K St. NW, Suite 600, Washington DC 20006; (800) 584-7336; *www.greenamericatoday.org*. See the online "Heal Your Home Center" at *www.greenamericatoday .org/go/healyourhome* for cleaning tips for the home, many of which apply to church use. Go to the *National Green Pages* at *www.greenamericatoday.org/pubs/greenpages* and search "cleaning products" for an extensive list of product sources.

- *Green Clean: The Environmentally Sound Guide to Cleaning Your Home,* by Linda Mason Hunter and Mikki Halpin (New York: Melcher Media, 2005). This guide and reference book for environmentally friendly cleaning includes recipes for making safe cleaning products.

◆ *Green This! Volume One: Greening Your Cleaning*, by Deirdre Imus (New York: Simon & Schuster, 2007). A practical guide on cleaning without possible or known carcinogens, neurotoxins, hormone disruptors, endocrine disruptors, ammonia, chlorine bleach, phosphates, formaldehyde, benzene, toluene, or petroleum-based ingredients.

◆ INFORM, 5 Hanover Square, Floor 19, New York, NY 10004; (212) 361-2400; *www.informinc.org*. This organization educates about health and environment issues and works to help people, businesses, and the government to adopt sustainable practices. Click on "Projects," then "Cleaning for Health" for related information. Also click on "Publications," then "Fact Sheets" for facts about toxic chemicals and health.

◆ Union of Concerned Scientists, 2 Brattle Square, Cambridge, MA 02238-9105; (617) 547-5552; *www.ucsusa.org/publications/greentips*. This nonprofit environmental organization uses independent scientific research coupled with citizen action to facilitate "changes in government policy, corporate practices and consumer choices." Click on "Greentips Archive," then on "Green Alternatives — Household Cleaners."

BUY FAIR TRADE COFFEE

Facts

◆ Coffee is one of the most heavily traded products in the world.

◆ 20 million people near the equator rely on coffee for their livelihood.

◆ Most small coffee farmers live in rural communities in poor countries in Latin America, Africa, and Asia, where they are isolated from the marketplace.

- Selling their product through "middlemen" who pay them the lowest prices they can results in a continuous cycle of hard work and poverty for the farmers.

- *Fair Trade* is an economic system of socially responsible companies buying products from small farmers (and other small businesses) at a fair price. Fair trade producers and producer cooperatives reinvest in their local communities, use environmentally friendly agriculture and business practices, and provide fair and safe labor conditions for workers.

- Faith communities were some of the initial supporters of fair trade products in the United States.

- Thousands of congregations serve and sell Fair Trade Certified coffee.

- Many religious denominations have *coffee projects* that provide educational literature, fundraising ideas, and bulk coffee buying programs.

- More than 80 percent of fair trade coffee is shade grown and organic.

- Shade grown coffee does not contribute to deforestation or loss of wildlife habitat.

- Fair trade companies also sell tea, cocoa, chocolate, and crafts.

- Additional fair trade products such as bananas, sugar, honey, olive oil, and vanilla are becoming available.

- Buying fair trade products advances a congregation's commitment to social, economic, and environmental justice.

—Information gathered from Green America,
Equal Exchange, and TransFair. See Resources below.

Actions

◆ Have a *forum or study group* on fair trade.

◆ *Educate* your congregation about the far-reaching positive effects of fair trade products on small farmers and their families around the world with bulletin inserts, posters, newsletter articles, and information and relevant links on your website.

◆ *Find denomination-specific information* on fair trade coffee projects at the Equal Exchange website.

◆ *Contact* Green America and Equal Exchange (see Resources) for educational and promotional materials.

◆ *Show* the Equal Exchange Interfaith Program video to your congregation.

◆ *Serve* Fair Trade Certified coffee and tea at church social hours and dinners.

◆ *Join* Green America's Fair Trade Alliance to receive on-going fair trade updates and resources, and to pledge your congregation's commitment to fair trade.

◆ *Encourage* church members to request fair trade coffee and tea at the grocery store and in coffee shops.

Resources

◆ Equal Exchange, 50 United Drive, W. Bridgewater, MA 02379; (774) 776-7366; *www.equalexchange.com*. This is the oldest (founded in 1986) and largest for-profit fair trade company in the United States. The company offers organic, gourmet, coffee, tea, cocoa, and other fair trade products. The website offers a fund-raising information kit and a quarterly online newsletter, *A Taste of Justice*. Their Interfaith Program partners with religious denominations to educate congregations and to promote the use of fair trade products in churches. It provides information about partner programs including the American Friends Service Committee Coffee Project, Church of the Brethren Coffee Project, Disciples of Christ Coffee Project, Lutheran World Relief Coffee Project, Presbyterian Coffee Project, and the United Methodist Committee on Relief Coffee Project.

♦ Fair Trade Federation (FTF), Hecker Center, Suite 107, 3025 Fourth St. NE, Washington, DC 20017-1102; (202) 636-3547; *www.fairtradefederation.org*. This is an international association of businesses and nonprofit organizations that are fully committed to fair trade. The FTF website provides information about World Fair Trade Day including a resource kit, Fair Trade Month, and Fair Trade Travel (tours that offer the opportunity to visit fair trade producers around the world).

♦ Fair Trade Labelling Organizations International (FLO), Bonne Talweg 177, 53129 Bonn, Germany; +49-228949230; *www.fairtrade.net*. A nonprofit association that sets the environmental, labor, and developmental standards for fair trade. TransFair USA is authorized by FLO to certify products in the United States.

♦ Green America, 1612 K St. NW, Suite 600, Washington DC 20006; (800) 584-7336; *www.greenamericatoday.org*. This not-for-profit membership organization focuses on using economic power to create a socially just and sustainable society. The website provides fair trade education and information. Their *Guide to Fair Trade* and their *National Green Pages*, a directory of "Eco-friendly, Socially Responsible Products and Services," can both be obtained in print versions or downloaded. Join the Fair Trade Alliance at *www.greenamericatoday.org/programs/fairtrade/alliance*.

♦ TransFair USA, 1500 Broadway, Suite 400, Oakland, CA 94612; (510) 663-5260; *www.transfairusa.org*. This nonprofit organization is the only third-party certifier of fair trade products in the United States. Their mission is to enable sustainable development and community empowerment through a more equitable global trade model that benefits farmers, workers, consumers, industry, and the Earth. Go to "Support Fair Trade," "Fair Trade and Faith." The website provides a downloadable guide entitled "Make Fair Trade Certified Coffee Your Congregation's Coffee of Choice," sample newsletter articles, a downloadable church bulletin insert, information about the certification process, FAQs, and other resources.

BUY FAIR TRADE COCOA AND CHOCOLATE

Facts

◆ 90 percent of the world's cocoa is grown on small family farms.

◆ $16 billion is generated in the cocoa industry each year, yet cocoa farmers' annual income generally averages less than $100 per household.

◆ Tens of thousands of child laborers are used on cocoa farms — some spraying pesticides and a high percentage not enrolled in school.

◆ Many of the cocoa farms are in open areas created by cutting down rainforests.

◆ Local water and soil is contaminated by farming methods that use pesticides, herbicides, and fungicides.

◆ Fair Trade Certified chocolate and cocoa ensures that small cocoa farmers receive a fair price and that safe labor practices and ecologically sound agricultural methods are used.

— Information gathered from Green America
and IITA. See Resources below.

Actions

* Have a *forum or study group* on fair trade.

* *Educate* your congregation about fair trade with bulletin insets, posters, newsletter articles, and information and relevant links on your website.

* *Contact* Lutheran World Relief Chocolate Project, Green America, Divine Chocolate, and other fair trade companies and projects (see the Resources section below) for educational and promotional materials.

* *Buy* Fair Trade Certified chocolate candy and cocoa.

* *Welcome new members* with a fair trade chocolate bar (and/or other fair trade products).

* *Serve* Fair Trade Certified hot chocolate at church social hours.

* *Join* Green America's Fair Trade Alliance to receive on-going fair trade updates and resources and to pledge your congregation's commitment to fair trade.

* *Have fundraisers* selling Fair Trade Certified chocolate candy and cocoa.

* *Have a Fair Trade Fair* or a Fair Trade Table selling fair trade chocolate (and other products) to raise awareness and promote social, economic, and environmental justice.

* *Encourage* church members to request fair trade chocolate at stores.

Resources

* Dagoba Organic Chocolate, 1105 Benson Way, Ashland, OR 97520; (800) 393-6075; *www.dagobachocolate.com*. This company follows "Full Circle Sustainability" principles of attention to "Quality, Ecology, Equity and Community [in] each step from cacao farms to our factory to you." Their

products are organic and sustainably grown chocolate, and some are Fair Trade Certified.

♦ Divine Chocolate Ltd., 4 Gainsford St., London SE1 2NE; *www.divinechocolate.com/home/default.aspx*. This fair trade chocolate company is co-owned by a cocoa farmers' cooperative in Ghana, whose members receive a fair price and also share in the company's profit. A nice feature on their website is the inclusion of photos, short biographies, and videos of farmers and their families; this furthers the company's objective of connecting the buyer with the farmer.

♦ Equal Exchange, 50 United Drive, W. Bridgewater, MA 02379; (774) 776-7366; *www.equalexchange.com*. This is the oldest (founded in 1986) and largest for-profit fair trade company in the United States. The company offers organic and gourmet cocoa and other fair trade products. The website offers a fund-raising information kit and a quarterly online newsletter, *A Taste of Justice*. Their Interfaith Program partners with religious denominations to educate congregations and to promote the use of fair trade products in churches.

♦ Green America, 1612 K St. NW, Suite 600, Washington DC 20006; (800) 584-7336; *www.greenamericatoday.org/ programs/fairtrade/products/chocolate.cfm*. This not-for-profit membership organization focuses on using economic power to create a socially just and sustainable society. The website provides fair trade education and information on chocolate, cocoa, tea, and other products; its *Guide to Fair Trade,* which can be obtained free in a print version or downloaded; the *National Green Pages*, a directory of "Eco-friendly, Socially Responsible Products and Services"; and the interesting and enlightening "Economic Action for Africa," *Co-op America Quarterly* no. 71 (Winter 2007), available in print and online.

- International Institute of Tropical Agriculture (IITA), *http://iita.org*. This Africa-based international research-for-development organization was established in 1967 and focuses on research to find solutions for hunger and poverty in Africa. See the 2002 IITA report on cocoa farm labor practices at *www.iita.org/cms/details/wpw-abts.pdf* (p. 26).

- Ithaca Fine Chocolates, 125 Heights Court, Ithaca, NY 14850; (607) 257-7954; *www.ithacafinechocolates.com*. This fair trade company sells chocolate "Art Bars" with a collectible card inside the wrapper featuring an art reproduction. Ten percent of the profits go to art education.

- Lutheran World Relief (LWR), Fair Trade Chocolate Project, 700 Light St., Baltimore, MD 21230; (410) 230-2800; *www.lwr.org/chocolate*. This LWR project works to put "faith into action" in Africa, Asia, the Middle East, and Latin America by creating solutions to poverty and injustice. In 2003 LWR launched its Chocolate Project to further promote fair trade in the United States, and in 2007 it became an investing partner in Divine Chocolate, a farmer-owned, fair trade company. LWR encourages parishes to sell and serve fair trade products, including chocolate.

- Yachana Gourmet, Vicente Solano 12–61 y Avenida Oriental, P.O. Box 17-17-185, Quito, Ecuador; (5932) 223–7278; *www.yachanagourmet.com/index.html*. This is an "ecologically conscious, socially progressive company designed to purchase agricultural commodities grown in the rain forest, add value to these products in the jungle, and open international markets." The company reinvests 100 percent of its profits in a nonprofit Ecuadorian foundation for rainforest preservation, environmental education, and local community development. It produces "Yachana Jungle Chocolate," which is 100 percent roasted cacao beans sweetened with sugar cane juice; it contains no other sugars, milk, cocoa powder, butters, lecithin, or artificial ingredients, and does not melt or require refrigeration.

USE BIODEGRADABLE
AND COMPOSTABLE DINNERWARE

Facts

- Many disposable plates, cups and utensils are made of petroleum-based plastic or polystyrene foam — neither of which is recyclable or biodegradable.

- Tens of billions of polystyrene plates and cups are disposed of every year.

- Polystyrene may leach toxic chemicals into food and beverages.

- Polystyrene and other plastics are a source of pollution and, once in the ocean, are eaten by marine animals, fish, and birds. This kills tens of thousands of marine animals each year.

- The vast majority of debris in the ocean is plastic.

- Some U.S. cities have banned polystyrene.

- Paper plates and cups will biodegrade, but are often made of virgin wood pulp.

- Paper makes up the largest portion (35 percent) of the municipal solid waste stream (EPA 2008a).

- Paper plates with up to 100 percent recycled paper content are available.

- Polystyrene, other plastics, and paper food containers and service ware often end up in landfills.

- In recent years, biodegradable and compostable plates, cups, utensils, and other food containers have become available.

- *Bioplastic* cups, utensils, and food containers are being made from bio-based materials (e.g., corn and potato starch).

- *Sugarcane* waste (bagasse) is being made into plates, bowls, cups, and food containers. Making these items from the sugarcane fiber pulp left after the juice is extracted avoids pollution caused by burning what was once considered to be waste.

- Bagasse and bioplastic ware are both made from tree-free, petroleum-free, and renewable sources.

- Biodegradable means the material will break down from the action of naturally occurring organisms.

- Compostable means it will break down in a compost site and leave no toxic waste.

- Bioplastic utensils and cups do not readily biodegrade or compost in home compost piles or in landfills; they need special composting facilities that are not available in many areas.

- Bagasse ware is compostable in home compost piles.

- Concerns about biodegradable and compostable ware include the use of petroleum-based energy in the planting and harvesting of source crops and in its manufacture and transport, as well as the use of pesticides on crops. It does, however, use less energy than petro-plastic, and it can totally biodegrade under the right conditions.

- Bioplastic technology continues to evolve.

- *Reusable kitchen ware* is generally the best option — though it takes water and energy to wash.

Actions

- *Reduce* the amount of disposable food service ware you use.

- *Avoid* using totally unnecessary plastic items such as straws and drinking cup lids.

- *Avoid* using polystyrene foam plates, cups, and containers.

- *Use, wash, and reuse* when you can.

- *Use (tree-free) biodegradable and compostable* dinnerware as an alternative to paper and petroleum-based plastic.

- *Compost* plates and containers that will break down in compost piles.

- *Search for and use a commercial compost facility* in your area (if available) for other compostable bioplastic products.

- *Continue to watch for growth and product improvement* in the bioplastics industry, and support the establishment of a separate waste-cycle stream for composting bioplastics.

Resources

- Biodegradable Products Institute, 331 West 57th St., Suite 415, New York, NY 10019; (888) 274-5646; *www.bpiworld.org*. This organization provides information about biodegradable products and along with the U.S. Composting Council uses the American Society for Testing and Materials (ASTM) specifications to certify products to use their "Compostable" logo.

- Find a Composter.com; *www.findacomposter.com*. This website of *BioCycle* magazine enables you to search by state or province, or zip or postal code for a commercial bioplastic composing facility.

- *Sources for purchasing* bioplastic, bagasse, and recycled paper food service products:

  > Biodegradable Store; *www.biodegradablestore.com*

  > The Green Office; *www.thegreenoffice.com* (Click on "Breakroom.")

  > Styrophobia; *www.styrophobia.com*

> Worldcentric; *www.worldcentric.org*. (Click on "Biocompostables," then "Frequently Asked Questions" for a good source of information on this topic.)

> Search "compostable plates and cups" online.

AVOID GREENWASHING

Facts

◆ As global warming and other environmental concerns draw ever more attention, environmentally friendly products and services are increasingly becoming available.

◆ Information about a company's practices, services, and products is helpful to consumers.

◆ However, insufficient, inaccurate, and irrelevant claims about a product's environmental impact are misleading.

◆ "Greenwashing" is a play on the word "whitewashing," which means to conceal faults and/or give a favorable impression or a falsely honorable and responsible appearance.

◆ Greenwashing then is whitewashing with regard to social and environmental effects.

◆ Greenwashing refers to a company, organization, or person inaccurately and disingenuously representing their product or message in pro-environment terms.

◆ Greenwashing is used to make products more attractive to buyers, sell more products, distract the public from past corporate misdeeds, falsely green a corporate image, divert the public and lawmakers from the need for regulatory laws, and secure approval for environmentally harmful corporate projects and practices.

◆ Not every product whose package or advertising features a nature scene or the words "green" or "natural" is Earth-friendly.

◆ Sophisticated greenwashing strategies can make responsible green purchasing difficult for the consumer. Fortunately resources are available to help us become informed consumers.

◆ Certification and logo programs exist to guide the consumer.

◆ "Single attribute" certification programs consider one environmental aspect of a product.

◆ "Multi-attribute" certification programs consider multiple environmental issues throughout the entire product lifecycle. These take into account the extraction of raw materials, the manufacturing process, the effects of product use, and ultimately recycling and disposal issues.

◆ Some certifications are more valuable and legitimate than others. Ones awarded by trade associations or individual manufacturers are suspect.

◆ The International Organization for Standardization (ISO) is a network of standards institutes of 157 countries (one per country). ISO 14024 standardizes eco-labeling.

◆ The U.S. member of ISO is the American National Standards Institute (ANSI), which accredits standards developers in the United States.

◆ Helpful and legitimate certification programs have:

> clear and rigorous standards

> third-party verification that standards are met

> ongoing evaluation for compliance

> public listings of certified products (TerraChoice 2007)

- By evaluating products and services, good certification programs provide shortcuts for green consumers.

- Helpful and legitimate certification programs are listed in the Resources section.

Actions

- *Pay attention* to claims and information about the products you purchase.

- *Watch for these greenwashing ploys* as identified by TerraChoice (2007):

  > *Hidden tradeoffs:* claims that a product is green based on only one or two factors, when in fact the larger environmental issues relating to the amount and kind of energy used in production and the pollution generated are ignored.

  > *No proof:* green claims that are not backed up by easily accessible evidence either on the package, through a provided telephone number, or on the company website.

  > *Vague claims:* too little or poorly defined information (e.g., a circle of arrows indicating "recycled," but with no information about which part of the product or the packaging contains recycled materials, or no information about the amount of pre-/post-consumer content of the recycled materials). Imprecise words with no substantiating evidence such as "green," "environmentally friendly," "natural," "recycled content," and "chemical-free" are also red flags.

  > *Irrelevant claims:* statements that are accurate but immaterial, e.g., products are still sometimes labeled "CFC-free,"

though all products are CFC-free because ozone depleting chlorofluorocarbons (CFC) have been banned from products for decades.

> *Inaccurate claims:* product claims for which no evidence is available. This is found infrequently. But if a product claims to be "certified organic" for instance, then the certification should be easily accessible and the certifier should be legitimate.

◆ *And watch for these ploys* as identified by Greenpeace (2008): A company that:

> publicizes an environmental program or product though the vast majority of its business operates in a decidedly anti-environmental way

> uses exaggerated green claims or spends more money on advertising their environmental achievements than they spend on actually doing the "achievement"

> publicizes green commitments at the same time they are lobbying against environmental laws or regulations

> advertises environmental "achievements" that are already mandated by law — trying to make their actions appear proactive or voluntary

◆ *Reduce* what you "need" to purchase.

◆ *Buy products that are certified by reputable certification programs* that make their standards and evaluation protocols clear and easily available for consumers to read and have developed their standards openly and publicly with input from a wide range of interested parties.

Resources

Certification Programs

- Chlorine Free Products Association (CFPA), 1304 South Main St., Algonquin, IL 60102; (847) 658-6104; *www .chlorinefreeproducts.org*. This not-for-profit organization accredits and sets standards for Totally Chlorine Free (TCF) and Processed Chlorine Free (PCF) products. Paper bleached with chlorine involves not only the use of that very toxic chemical but also the use of large quantities of water. Click on "Labeling Marks" to see their logos and read the criteria. TCF paper is made with no recycled content, but can be made tree-free (e.g., with kenaf or hemp). PCF certified paper must contain at least 30 percent post-consumer recycled content. See the website for other criteria for certification.

- EcoLogo Program, c/o TerraChoice Environmental Marketing, 171 Nepean St., Suite 400, Ottawa, Ontario K2P 0B4; (800) 478-0399; *www.ecologo.org*. This multi-attribute program awards their logo (three stylized birds that overlap to form a leaf) to products and services that are "environmentally preferable" to other products in the same category. The program evaluates the entire lifecycle of the product. Products and services by category are listed on the website, as are criteria for certification. TerraChoice manages this program.

- Forest Stewardship Council (FSC); *www.fscus.org*. This organization accredits independent certifiers to evaluate and certify forests using FSC standards, which promote responsible management of forests around the world. Click on "Standards and Policies" to read their "Principles and Criteria." The FSC logo (a combination of a checkmark and a tree) on wood and paper products indicates certification.

- Green-e, c/o Center for Resource Solutions, P.O. Box 29512, Presidio Building 97, Arguello Boulevard, San Francisco, CA

94129; (415) 561-2100; *www.green-e.org*. This organization certifies sources of renewable electricity and renewable energy certificates (REC). They also certify carbon offsets through their Green-e Climate program. RECs are different from carbon offsets in that offsets represent new renewable energy that displaces fossil fuel energy and so results in a reduction of GHG emissions; RECs represent a quantity of renewable energy produced. Click on "Buy Green-e Certified," "Renewable Energy for Your Organization," then enter your state and what kind of renewable energy you want to buy, and a list of vendors will appear.

◆ Greenguard Environmental Institute (GEI); *greenguard.org*. This nonprofit organization establishes indoor air quality standards and is a third-party certifier for products, environments, and buildings. Click on "Find Products" for a list of certified products in such categories as adhesives, cleaning products, ceiling systems, doors, floor finishes, paints, insulation, and others.

◆ Green Seal, 100 Connecticut Ave. NW, Suite 827, Washington, DC 20036-5525; (202) 872-6400; *www.greenseal.org*. This nonprofit organization certifies products and services; these are listed on the website. This is a multi-attribute certification program.

Other Related Resources

◆ American National Standards Institute (ANSI), *www.ansi.org*. ANSI accredits standards developers in the United States.

◆ Greenpeace, *stopgreenwash.org*. This website was started in 2008 by Greenpeace to focus on identifying, exposing, and challenging greenwashing campaigns by companies, and to give the public and lawmakers the "information and tools they need to confront corporate deception, to look beneath this green veneer and hold corporations accountable for the impacts [they] are having on our planet." See their greenwashing criteria (page 76 above). The website provides examples of specific corporations' campaigns and greenwashing ads (including videos).

◆ TerraChoice Environmental Marketing Inc., 2 Penn Center Plaza, Suite 200, 1500 JFK Boulevard, Philadelphia, PA 19102; (800) 478-0399; *www.terrachoice.com*. TerraChoice manages the EcoLogo certification program and publishes the online Green Paper Report, "The Six Sins of Greenwashing: A Study of Environmental Claims in North American Consumer Markets."

Chapter Four

Worship and Services

Environmental stewardship is woven throughout the entire fabric of a church. Other sections of this book address the workings of buildings, landscaping the grounds, ramifications of purchasing particular products, and a variety of additional environment-related topics. Fundamental to the functioning of any church is worship, and so we now take a look at ways to cast a green hue on our services.

Many denominations have statements, calls to action, and programs specifically related to the faith–environment connection. In addition, several Christian relief agencies and interfaith partnership organizations are partially or wholly focused on faith–environment issues and actions. In fact, the amount of information and resources available is astounding. These wonderful resources make incorporating environmental stewardship messages and actions into worship relatively easy. Some of the ones most relevant to worship are listed in Resources in each of the following Action sections. Others are listed throughout this book. Especially take note of the Internet links in the Resources section under Websites.

Celebrating Earth Day in church is probably the most obvious way to inter-weave faith and the environment in worship. But this is only one of a multitude of ways to bring an environmental stewardship message into religious services. Messages about our responsibility to God's creation and about our roles as guardians and keepers of the Earth can be integrated into a variety of services. And our actions can then reflect these messages.

This chapter provides **Facts**, **Actions**, and **Resources** for greening sermons, using related prayers and songs, and celebrating Earth Day. It also covers ways to entwine environmental stewardship messages and actions into baptisms, weddings, and funerals. By doing this we deepen our spiritual connections — to each other, to the Earth, and to God.

SERMONS

Facts

- Environmental stewardship can be the focus of sermons and be briefly mentioned in other sermons.

- Resources are available for assisting in creation care sermon development.

- Lay persons with expertise in environment issues or in the interconnectedness of religious faith and environmental stewardship can be interesting guest preachers or speakers.

Actions

- *Explore* faith–environment resources.

- *Contact your denomination* at the national level for their support and resources.

- *Invite lay persons* from the congregation, local environmental groups, Interfaith Power and Light, or your denomination's environmental projects to be preachers or speakers.

- *Invite pastors* from other churches to preach on faith and the environment and to share their churches' environmental stewardship practices and changes.

- *Incorporate faith–environment phrases* throughout a typical service (e.g., "as good stewards of God's creation"; "protecting and restoring the Earth"; "tending the garden"; "caring for all that God created"; "living lightly on the Earth so that our human family worldwide can simply live"; "social justice and Earth justice"; "eco-faith").

- *Consider these topics* for sermons:

  > the biblical call for environmental stewardship

  > theology, morality, and ecology

  > water: the worldwide crisis and its link to our actions and to poverty

  > hunger: its connection to poverty and global warming

  > farms, food, and faith

  > Lent: giving up something that really matters

  > Thanksgiving: thanks be to God for the gifts of the Earth

  > Christmas: rethink, reduce, reuse, recycle, rejoice

Resources

- Creation Care for Pastors, Evangelicals & Scientists United to Protect Creation, *creationcareforpastors.com.* This is "a bridge building effort between top environmental scientists and evangelical leaders." Many resources are available on the website including video and text versions of Creation Care sermons.

- Earth Ministry, 6512 Twenty-third St., Suite 317, Seattle, WA 98117; (206) 632-2426; *www.earthministry.org.* This organization's mission is "to inspire and mobilize the Christian community to play a leadership role in building a just and sustainable future." Go to *www.earthministry.org/ Congregations/sermons.htm* for sample sermons. Their *Greening Congregations Handbook*, by T. M. Barnett (Seattle: Earth

Ministry, 2002) provides worship ideas, suggestions, and resources (see pp. 9–14 of section 3).

* National Religious Partnership for the Environment, 49 S. Pleasant St., Suite 301, Amherst, MA 01002; (413) 253-1515; *www.nrpe.org*. This is an association of the U.S. Conference of Catholic Bishops, the National Council of Churches U.S.A., the Coalition on the Environment and Jewish Life, and the Evangelical Environmental Network. The website offers "resources and accounts of how people of faith are acting upon God's mandate to be stewards of our precious Earth," perspectives and teachings from different religious traditions, and scriptures that speak to creation care.

* *Preaching Creation throughout the Church Year,* by J. M. Phillips (Boston: Cowley Publications, 2000). This book links scripture and care of creation. It is organized around the three-year lectionary cycle and is useful for planning sermons and lessons.

* Presbyterian Hunger Program, (888) 728-7228; *www.pcusa .org/hunger/features/climate*. This Presbyterian Church (USA) program provides an adult study guide as well as resource material to introduce children to the issue of world hunger. It includes suggestions for hunger-related hymns and songs and offers educational and curriculum booklets (e.g., *Just Eating? Practicing Our Faith at the Table; Is There Enough?: A New Children's Curriculum on Hunger*).

* Web of Creation: Ecology Resources Transforming Faith and Society, (262) 633-5438; *www.webofcreation.org*. This website of the Lutheran School of Theology at Chicago is a rich source of information for congregations striving to become green. Among many other resources, it provides an eighty-six-page *Training Manual for the Green Congregation Program.* Litanies, prayers, sample sermons, and sample

services (including blessing of the animals and tree planting services) are available on this website. It is an excellent source of information for congregations.

PRAYERS AND HYMNS

Facts

* Prayers, litanies, hymns, and other songs with themes of creation, nature, caring for others, and gratitude add breadth and beauty to worship services.

Actions

* *Include these prayers, hymns, and readings* in worship services.

* *Search Resources* below to access materials.

* *Write personal prayers* for Earth healing and share them during worship.

* *Encourage other creative expression* of creation care (e.g., liturgical dance, skits, banners).

Resources

* Earth Ministry, 6512 Twenty-third St., Suite 317, Seattle, WA 98117; (206) 632-2426; *www.earthministry.org*. Click on "Cultivate Congregational Involvement," then "Worship Aids" for a wealth of resources. Earth Ministry has prayers on its website from the 1990 UN Environmental Sabbath/Earth Rest Day publication, *Only One Earth*. These short and beautiful prayers of awareness, sorrow, healing, and gratitude are available at *www.earthministry.org/Congregations/UN_Sabbath.htm*. The print version is in Earth Ministry's *Greening Congregations Handbook,* by T. M. Barnett (Seattle: Earth Ministry, 2002), Appendix H. The *Handbook* also supplies a "Song Bibliography" of "creation-honoring songs and hymns."

- *Earth Prayers from around the World: 365 Prayers, Poems, and Invocations for Earth,* edited by E. Roberts and E. Amidon (San Francisco: HarperCollins, 1991, 1993). This book includes prayers, verses, chants, and songs from many cultures.

- Web of Creation: Ecology Resources Transforming Faith and Society, (262) 633-5438; *www.webofcreation.org.* The Lutheran School of Theology at Chicago website provides many resources including litanies, blessings, prayers (including "Praying with Creation" prayers that correspond to the church calendar) and links to other resources.

ADULT STUDY GROUPS

Facts

- Offering adult study groups as an adjunct to worship services and Sunday school classes provides an opportunity for church members to gather and explore specific topics that otherwise might not be a part of church services or activities.

- Topics related to the interrelationship of religious faith and environmental stewardship are many and varied and are well-suited to group study and discussion.

Actions

- *Organize* time-limited (one to eight weeks) study and discussion groups around a specific topic.

- *Publicize* the adult study group topic in the church bulletin, newsletter, and website, as well as in community publications to attract other than church members.

- *Ask someone to facilitate the group* who is knowledgeable about or interested in the topic.

◆ *Suggested topics:*

> *Book review* by a facilitator, or *book discussion.* For recommended books see Resources.

> *Carbon Fast for Lent:* This could occur a couple of weeks prior to Lent or during the weeks of Lent. Participants can study aspects of climate change and the relationship between global warming, religion, mission relief efforts, poverty, and hunger; the value of a carbon fast; and the ways to incorporate carbon-reducing measures into one's life. For more information see Fast from Carbon for Lent (page 147 below).

> *Creating a Truly Green Christmas in Our Church:* Explore and plan ways to celebrate the holidays by integrating social and ecological justice with peace on Earth and the true meaning of Christmas. For ways to do this see the Green Christmas action section (page 149 below).

> *Fair Trade:* Provide education about fair trade; use available resource materials to facilitate awareness; discuss the related social, economic, and environmental issues; and consider ways of bringing fair trade products to the congregation. Refer to the Buy Fair Trade sections in the "Products" chapter (pages 65 and 69 above).

> *Steps to Greening Our Church:* Brainstorm and plan for moving the church toward more environmental stewardship practices.

> *The Holy Land:* Reenvision all land as holy. Discuss why all the lands (and water and air) of the Earth are sacred. *Share personal photos* and stories of natural places.

> Any other theology–ecology topics suggested by someone willing to facilitate.

Resources

* *The Body of God: An Ecological Theology*, by Sallie McFague (Minneapolis: Augsburg Fortress, 1993). This book focuses on the model of the universe as God's body and on multiple theological issues including creation and the natural world from this perspective.

* *The Earth Bible* volumes: *Readings from the Perspective of the Earth; The Earth Story in Genesis; The Earth Story in Wisdom Traditions; The Earth Story in the Psalms and the Prophets; The Earth Story in the New Testament,* by Norman C. Habel (Cleveland: Pilgrim Press). These volumes are the work of international biblical scholars who write about selected sections of the Bible from an Earth perspective.

* *The Green Bible: New Revised Standard Version* (HarperOne, 2008). This Bible highlights the scriptures that relate to creation care. It also includes essays and resources.

* *Greening Congregations Handbook: Stories, Ideas, and Resources for Cultivating Creation Awareness and Care in Your Congregation,* edited by Tanya Marcovna Barnett (Seattle: Earth Ministry, 2002). This spiral-bound book of suggestions and resources from Earth Ministry focuses on the northwest United States, but much of the book is applicable to other churches and regions.

* *Loving Nature: Ecological Integrity and Christian Responsibility,* by James A. Nash (Nashville: Abingdon Press, 1991). This book explores an ethical perspective on the environmental crisis and its relationship to Christianity. The author draws the connections between social justice, ecological justice, and peace.

* National Council of Churches Eco-Justice Programs, 110 Maryland Ave. NE, Suite 108, Washington, DC 20002; (202) 544-2350; *nccecojustice.org./about.html*. This program

of the National Council of Churches of Christ works with denominations "to protect and restore God's Creation." It provides information, education, an "Activist's Toolbox" of environmental stewardship actions, links to multiple denominational and faith-based environmental resources and online downloadable resources.

+ Prayers of Light and Color, *www.prayersoflightandcolor.com.* The photo "images of God's Creation and Creatures" on this website of minister and photographer Dwight Morita can prompt faith–environment "sacred conversations" and inspire others to artistically capture scenes of nature and life and share them in the group.

+ *The Sacred Balance: Rediscovering Our Place in Nature,* by David Suzuki, 3rd ed. (Vancouver, B.C.: Greystone Books, 2007). This book was written by a leading environmentalist and co-founder of the David Suzuki Foundation in Vancouver, British Columbia. Originally published in 1997, this classic work discusses how we can live a just and sustainable life and at the same time meet our physical and spiritual needs.

+ *Saving God's Green Earth: Rediscovering the Church's Responsibility to Environmental Stewardship,* by Tri Robinson (Norcross, Ga.: Ampelon Publishing, 2006). This book was written to encourage Christians to "embrace the biblical mandate to care for creation."

+ *Science, Soul, and the Spirit of Nature,* by Irene van Lippe-Biesterfeld (Rochester, Vt.: Bear & Company, 2005). The author interviews twelve visionaries from all the world's continents about human connection to the Earth.

+ *Serve God, Save the Planet: A Christian Call to Action,* by J. Matthew Sleeth (White River Junction, Vt.: Chelsea Green Publishing, 2006). This is a particularly well written and readable book written by a physician about his journey from living the "American dream" lifestyle to drastically reducing his family's ecological footprint. He makes a clear and convincing case for the Christians' responsibility in caring for environment.

CELEBRATE EARTH DAY

Facts

◆ Earth Day was first celebrated in 1970; in fact, two Earth Days occurred that year — one on the spring equinox (March 21) and one on April 22.

◆ Earth Day is generally now celebrated on April 22.

◆ Earth Day Sunday is celebrated in churches on the Sunday closest to April 22.

◆ Celebrating Earth Day in church is just one way to focus attention on environmental stewardship and caring for all of God's creation.

Actions

◆ *Plan an Earth Day celebration service.*

◆ *Use Earth Day resources* available from the National Council of Churches or other resources.

◆ *Develop your own unique celebration.*

◆ *Consider incorporating some of the following into your service:*

> a sermon linking everyday actions to worldwide issues of the environment, poverty, and hunger

> a guest speaker on a relevant environmental topic

> hymns, prayers, and responsive readings with nature themes

> skits involving members of the congregation that address an environmental issue

> a photo slideshow of nature's beauty (possibly by church members)

> a photo slideshow of past "green" church initiatives and activities

> a photo slideshow of church members engaging in "green" actions (e.g., riding a bike to the store, recycling cans, gardening, mowing the grass with a reel mower, building a compost pile, harvesting vermicast, hanging clothes on the line).

♦ *Include children* of the congregation in the Earth Day service.

♦ *Document and publicize* Earth Day activities through the church newsletter and website, and in the local newspaper.

♦ *Make an offering to the Earth* by planting a tree or flowers near the church or in a local park; organizing a group to adopt a highway; or earmarking funds (or taking up a special collection) to make a donation to a local, national, or international environmental organization. See "Make an Offering to the Earth" in the next section.

♦ *Submit accounts of your Earth Day activities* to the National Council of Churches Eco-Justice program and to your denomination's journal or environmental program.

Resources

♦ Earth Day Network (EDN), *ww2.earthday.net*. EDN was founded by the originators of Earth Day in 1970. Their mission is to grow and mobilize the environmental movement worldwide to promote "a healthy, sustainable planet." Click on "EDN Programs and Events," then on "Religious and Faith Communities Outreach" or *ww2.earthday.net/~earthday/node/73*. They encourage ministers to sign their Pulpit Pledge to agree to preach on global climate change. The website provides Earth Day and other environment-related resources, as well as "pulpit resources."

♦ National Council of Churches of Christ Eco-Justice Programs, *www.nccecojustice.org*. Each year the NCC Eco-Justice Working Group focuses on a specific environmental issue for Earth Day. The website provides educational materials for children and adults, suggestions as to ways congregations can celebrate Earth Day, relevant biblical references, and "sermon starters."

♦ Sierra Club, Environmental Partnerships Programs, Faith and the Environment, *www.sierraclub.org/partnerships/faith*. According to the Sierra Club, almost half of their members regularly attend religious services. The Club supports the partnering of their volunteers with people of faith to address environmental issues. The website provides links to religion–environment articles and to many faith-related environmental websites.

♦ Children's books:

> *Earth Day: Rookie Read-About Holidays,* by Trudi Strain Trueit (New York: Children's Press, 2006).

> *It's Earth Day!* by Mercer Mayer (New York: HarperFestival, 2008).

> *The Lorax by Dr. Seuss,* by Theodor Seuss Geisel (New York: Random House, 1971).

> *The Three R's: Reuse, Reduce, Recycle,* by Nuria Roca (Hauppauge, N.Y.: Barron's Educational Series, 2007).

MAKE AN OFFERING TO THE EARTH

Facts

- Collection of offerings occurs weekly in churches.

- For Earth Day or other celebrations, symbolic and tangible offerings to the Earth can be incorporated into the service.

- Daily we take from the Earth, in the form of water, food, air, oil, coal, gas, and trees; an "Earth Offering" allows us to give back to that which sustains us.

Actions

Choose a type of Earth Offering:

- *A donation to an environmental organization* in the church's name

  > Choose a local or national organization whose work supports your churches' green mission.

  > Earmark church mission money, or collect a special offering, for the donation.

  > Give a brief description of the recipient organization and their work during worship service.

- Individual offerings and pledges from church members

  > *Make pledge cards* that read: "As my offering to the Earth, I pledge _____ ."

  > *Distribute the pledge cards the week prior* to the service, and ask members to consider making a commitment to give back to the Earth in some way.

  > *Provide examples* such as: I pledge to... turn off my lights when I'm not in the room;... research energy-efficient

vehicle options for my next car;...work in the church garden one day each month;...buy and use canvas grocery bags when I shop;...take my own reusable cup to the coffee shop;...turn the church compost pile every two weeks;...contribute X dollars to the church fund for photovoltaic panels. If you have a specific green church project that needs funding, make pledge cards that read "I pledge to donate $_____ to the [*name the project*] fund."

> *Collect the pledge cards* in a special collection plate during the regular offering. Or alternatively, have people hang their cards on a small potted tree to decorate it, make it part of the celebration, and enable others to peruse the pledges following the service.

> Keep a separate record of pledge monies as they are received, and apply this money toward the designated projects.

BAPTIZE BABY GREEN

Facts

◆ Many Christian churches practice the rite of infant baptism.

◆ When a baby is baptized, he or she is initiated into the Christian community.

◆ Water, a precious natural resource, is used in baptism.

◆ Though we often ignore the fact that an increasing world population is one of the major environmental problems we face — it is true.

◆ Every person on the Earth leaves a "footprint" and contributes to global warming.

◆ U.S. babies add way more than their fair share of greenhouse gases.

♦ According to the Carbon Dioxide Information Analysis Center (CDIAC), in 2004, per capita carbon emissions* in the United States were 5.61 metric tons.

♦ In contrast, the annual carbon emissions in metric tons per person of other nations:

Canada	5.46	Botswana	0.66
Australia	4.41	Zimbabwe	0.22
Japan	2.69	Senegal	0.12
Germany	2.67	Uganda	0.02
Mexico	1.14	Cambodia	0.01
China (mainland)	1.05		

♦ The carbon emissions of a baby born in the United States are (in 2004 numbers) approximately equal to the carbon emissions of:

2 Japanese children	47 Senegalese children
5 Chinese children	281 Ugandan children
26 Zimbabwean children	561 Cambodian children

♦ Acknowledging a child's impact on the Earth at the time of baptism and addressing it directly begins a tradition of fostering love and a sense of responsibility for God's creation, and it can be very appropriately incorporated into a baptism.

---

*Data related to "carbon emissions" or "CO_2 emissions" might appear to vary considerably from source to source. This is due to variations in *units measured* and the way in which it is reported. CDIAC measures only the *carbon* in the CO_2 molecule. In contrast, the UN Statistics Division website reports *carbon + oxygen* (CO_2). According to T. J. Blasing at CDIAC (personal communication, June 4, 2008), the CO_2 molecule is 44/12 (or 3.667) heavier than the carbon molecule. So, for example, the per person average U.S. *carbon emission* = 5.61 metric tons and the average CO_2 *emission* = 20.6 metric tons (i.e., 5.61 x 44/12 = 20.6). So if you see emissions reported as *carbon* emissions, multiply the number by 3.667 to calculate the CO_2 emissions.

Actions

- *Provide the opportunity* for parents to green their baby's baptism.

- *Include an environmental message in the baptism service: Suggested phrases* for inclusion:

  > "As this precious gift from God is welcomed into our church, a gift from this child's family is given to God's creation."

  > "As we thank God for this new life, we plant new life in the Earth."

  > "We offer prayers of hope for smaller footprints on the Earth."

  > "As this child grows, may her footprint on God's Earth remain small."

  > "As we nurture this child, so let us nurture the planet."

  > "Small feet can make large carbon footprints. This child's family is taking steps to reduce theirs and their baby's footprints on the Earth."

  > "This child and our Earth have things in common — both are beautiful, fragile, God's creations, and in need of our nurturing."

- *Make a direct offering to the Earth: Suggested family actions:*

  > Plant a tree in honor of the baby on the church grounds, or have a tree planted in a park or forest through a city, county, state, national, or private program.

  > Calculate the anticipated carbon emissions of the child for a year, or a lifetime, and buy equivalent carbon offsets.

> Calculate the anticipated carbon emissions of the child and donate to the church's own carbon offset (or other environmental) fund (see "Carbon Calculators" on page 31 above).

> If space permits on church grounds, plant a tree in a grove of trees donated in honor or memory.

> On a smaller scale, donate plants to an established, but ever expanding, children's garden on the church grounds.

> Donate to an environmental organization in the baby's name.

◆ *Make any baptism-related social celebration environmentally friendly.*

> See related Actions throughout this book related to food, paper use, decorations, dinnerware, reducing, reusing, recycling, and zero waste.

Resources

◆ All Things Green, *www.allthingsgreen.net/marketplace/index .php*. Click on "Baby and Toddler," then "Carbon Offsets" to be inspired by this UK site that enables people to purchase offsets (in pounds) of trees planted in India and Africa to counterbalance carbon emissions related to their use of disposable diapers.

◆ Carbon Dioxide Information Analysis Center (CDIAC), Oak Ridge National Laboratory, U.S. Department of Energy, Oak Ridge, Tennessee; (865) 574-0390. This is the primary climate change data and information analysis center for the U.S. Department of Energy. For statistics related to carbon emissions by country, click on *cdiac.ornl.gov/trends/emis/tre_coun.html,* then on "World's Countries Ranked by 2004 fossil fuel CO_2 Per Capita Emission Rates."

+ "Green Baby Steps for the Future of the Planet" (John Laumer, 2007) on the Treehugger website at *www.treehugger.com/files/ 2007/09/green_baby_step.php*. This is an article about a couple in Budapest, Hungary, who calculated the expected lifetime carbon footprint of their baby girl born in August 2007 and arranged for approximately three hundred trees to be planted in a new and protected "climate forest" in northeastern Hungary.

GREEN WEDDINGS

Facts

+ Over 2 million weddings occur in the United States annually (Association for Wedding Professionals International 2008).

+ The average cost is in excess of $27,000 (Anderson 2007).

+ A typical wedding unnecessarily consumes many resources and generates much waste.

+ Many couples are opting for greener weddings.

+ Churches can help couples plan environmentally and socially responsible weddings.

Actions

+ *Provide resources* that educate brides and grooms on the issues and encourage them to consider having eco-friendly ceremonies and receptions.

+ *Provide these suggestions to save energy, transportation fuel, and other resources:*

> Have the wedding during a time of year and time of day when no heating of air conditioning will be necessary, or have an outdoor wedding.

> Send invitations by email, personalized wedding website, or on recycled or tree-free paper.

> Reduce fuel use by having the wedding and reception in the same place.

> Wear rented, borrowed, vintage, or locally made, natural fiber clothes.

> Use beeswax or vegetable-based (instead of petroleum-based) candles.

> Include phrases in wedding vows that indicate commitment to caring for creation.

> Participate in a wedding gift registry that enables guests to donate to the couple's favorite environmental causes.

> Donate to environmental causes instead of giving favors.

> Support local businesses and artisans: give favors of locally grown and locally made edible or useful nonplastic items (e.g., jams, candy, flower seeds, small plants, bookmarks made of reclaimed scrap wood).

> Hire caterers who do not use throwaway plates, utensils, or serving dishes.

> Eliminate pesticide pollution by buying organic flowers and food.

> Keep decorations simple and natural; use fewer and local flowers.

> Showcase seasonal local produce or greenery for centerpieces.

> Let the season and your geographic region dictate your menu.

> Support local farmers; serve locally grown organic food if possible.

> Serve Marine Stewardship Council certified fish, antibiotic-free poultry, and organic beef.

> Serve organic wine.

> Serve fair trade coffee.

> Provide birdseed to be thrown instead of rice.

> Plan eco-friendly honeymoon travel; purchase carbon offsets for travel or honeymoon close to home.

◆ *Plant a tree* on the church grounds to commemorate the wedding.

Resources

◆ *Achieve Green: Eco-Weddings,* by Tiffany Green (Tynan's Independent Media, 2008).

◆ Changing the Present, *changingthepresent.org/weddings.* This nonprofit website enables couples to register so that wedding guests can make donations in the names of the bride and groom, and "[change] the world, one gift at a time." A wide variety of charities are represented, including many that focus on environmental issues.

◆ *Eco-chic Weddings: Simple Tips to Plan an Environmentally Friendly, Socially Responsible, Affordable, and Stylish Celebration,* by Emily E. Anderson (Long Island City, N.Y.: Hatherleigh, 2007).

◆ *The Everything Green Wedding Book: Plan an Elegant, Affordable, Earthfriendly Wedding,* by Wenona Napolitano (Avon, Mass.: Adams Media, 2008).

◆ *Organic Weddings: Balancing Ecology, Style and Tradition* by Michelle Kozin (Gabriola Island, B.C.: New Society Publishers, 2003).

◆ World Wildlife Fund (WWF), 1250 Twenty-Fourth St. NW, P.O. Box 97180, Washington, DC 20090-7180; (202) 293-4800; WWF Weddings & Celebrations, *www.justgive.org/*

worldwildlifefund/weddings/index.jsp. Couples can create a wedding registry page to send to guests who can choose to make donations to WWF as their wedding gift. Couples can also make donations in guests' names for conservation purposes instead of giving favors. The site provides a list of "Green Wedding Tips" and information on planning an "eco-honeymoon" through WWF's Travel Partners.

NATURAL FUNERALS

Facts

- Each year in the United States, millions of burials occur and billions of dollars are spent on funerals.

- Typical U.S. funerals involve formaldehyde embalming fluid, hardwood and steel caskets, concrete vaults, and quarried stone markers.

- Estimated amounts buried in the United States annually:

  > 827,060 gallons of embalming fluid

  > 90,272 tons of steel

  > 2,700 tons of copper and bronze

  > 30 million board feet of hardwoods

  > 1,636,000 tons of reinforced concrete

  > 14,000 tons of steel
  >   — Glendale Memorial Nature Preserve, 2007

- Using a funeral home, enclosing a coffin in a burial vault, and embalming (at least within twenty-four hours) are not required by law (Funeral Consumers Alliance 2007).

- Hundreds of environmentally friendly cemeteries exist in Great Britain.

- A movement toward "green" cemeteries and funerals is growing in the United States.

- Greening the funeral process reduces the negative environmental impact.

- A green funeral can cost from several hundred dollars to several thousand dollars; a conventional modest funeral generally costs $6000–10,000 or more.

- The Green Burial Council, in collaboration with landscape architects, consumer advocates, and the Trust for Public Land, has recently developed standards for natural and conservation burial grounds, funeral homes, caskets, and cremation.

- Burials can be in forest reserves.

- Green funerals are actually a return to traditional U.S. funerals prior to the mid-nineteenth century.

- Lower costs, the natural beauty of sites, the avoidance of toxic chemicals, and land preservation make green funerals an attractive alternative to conventional funerals.

- Planning ahead enables people to make their last earthly acts green ones.

Actions

- *Research green funeral options and provide access* to this information for church members. *Suggest:*

  > home or church funerals

  > living memorials (e.g., a tree) or a small natural engraved or plain indigenous stone instead of marble or granite grave markers.

  > donations to the deceased's favorite environmental group in lieu of cut flowers.

> biodegradable casket and natural fiber shroud.

> personal oral remembrances and tributes that speak of the person's love of nature and care for the environment.

Resources

♦ Celebration Forest, P.O. Box 3005, Bonners Ferry, ID, 83805; (877) 245-7378; *www.celebrationforest.com*. To recognize a special occasion or to honor the memory of someone who has died, this company will plant a memorial tree in a designated place in a protected forest. The forest preserve was started by a professional forester.

♦ Ecoffins, *www.ecoffins.co.uk*. This English company offers coffins made of pine, bamboo, and willow. The website has beautiful photos, and even a carbon calculator to determine the amount of carbon emission generated in shipping a bamboo coffin from where it is (fair trade) made in China

♦ Fernwood, 301 Tennessee Valley Rd., Mill Valley, CA 94941; (415) 383-7100; *www.foreverfernwood.com*. This is a thirty-two-acre site where natural burials involve no toxic embalming fluids or concrete vaults, and where only biodegradable caskets or burial shrouds are used. Natural and plant markers are permitted, and graves can be located with Global Positioning System (GPS) coordinates.

♦ Final Passages, P.O. Box 1721, Sebastopol, CA 95473; (707) 824-0268; *www.finalpassages.org*. This project provides education about "personal and legal rights concerning home or family-directed funerals and... burial and cremation." They offer a guide entitled *Creating Home Funerals*.

♦ Funeral Consumers Alliance, 22 Patchen Rd., South Burlington, VT 05403; (800) 765-0107; *www.funerals.org*. This is a nonprofit "dedicated to protecting a consumer's right to choose a meaningful, dignified, affordable funeral." They offer pamphlets and newsletters on funeral options and information about funerals without funeral home involvement.

◆ Glendale Memorial Nature Preserve, 297 Railroad Ave., DeFuniak Springs, FL 32433; (850) 859-2141; online at *www.glendalenaturepreserve.org.* Their goal is "to enhance, protect, and preserve a valuable area of distinctive beauty, provide affordable, environmentally sensible burial options, and to encourage a return to sane, older, traditional approaches to burial." They have burial and cremation repository sites where they ban vaults and toxic embalming chemicals, and allow only biodegradable caskets and urns. Natural fiber shrouds and blankets are permitted, and markers are natural stone, living trees, or other plants.

◆ Green Burial Council, 550 D St. Michaels Drive, Santa Fe, NM 87508; (888) 966-3330; *www.greenburialcouncil.org.* This organization has collaborated with consumer advocates, landscape architects, and persons involved in the public land trusts to develop a certification program for cemeteries, funeral homes, caskets, urns, and cremation. The website lists the standards.

◆ Memorial Ecosystems, 111 West Main St., Westminster, SC 29693; (864) 647-7798; *www.memorialecosystems.com.* This preserve was founded in 1996 "to harness the funeral industry for land protection and restoration." It currently has two memorial nature preserves (one in South Carolina and one in Georgia), and plans to eventually have a million acres of "wild-lands" devoted to "environmentally and socially responsible death care."

Chapter Five

Finances

If your church has financial investments, then examining the types of stocks and funds in the portfolio is incumbent upon church leaders and other members of the congregation. Environmental stewardship permeates the whole of a green church — the policies, purchases, and practices. Just as the paper you buy, the temperature at which you set the thermostat, and the way you landscape all reflect your congregation's level of commitment to caring for creation, so does the way you spend, save, and invest the church's money.

Throughout this book are ways suggested to decrease spending by reducing what we "need" and by using and conserving what we have. This chapter focuses on the money that is *not* spent on purchases. The following Action sections look at greening investments, suggest a creative way to accumulate money for a renewable energy project at the church, and recommend designating and donating some monies specifically to environmental causes.

Many stocks and mutual funds finance industries, products, and practices that are at odds with the stated values of a church. Examining the church's financial holdings can lead to divesting of ones that are antithetical to your congregation's values, and investing in ones that reflect them. An efficient way of doing this is by investing in socially responsible mutual funds. Socially responsible investing (SRI) allows you to choose funds that reflect your desired environmental and social interests. Screening funds on your own can be difficult and off-putting. Researching the practices of every company is labor- and time-intensive, and therefore often does not get done. However, socially responsible funds have been screened to eliminate certain types of industries and products, and you can choose ones that have eliminated companies that contribute to global warming and environmental degradation. The Resources section guides you in the process of leading your church to becoming an environmentally responsible investor. A green church changes more than light bulbs; it also changes investments.

Building on the concept of carbon neutrality, churches can set up their own carbon offsets fund to finance a home-grown renewable energy project. If your church wants to install some photo voltaic panels, for example, a church carbon offsets fund might be the answer to funding it. This chapter walks you through the whys and ways of doing this. And finally, an easy way to take a step in the creation care direction is to ensure that some church monies are donated to those close to home or in developing countries who are furthering Earth care through their environmental projects.

The **Facts, Actions,** and **Resources** in this chapter are a guide to encourage congregations to use their economic power for the Earth. Whether the amounts are large or small, encourage one another to spend, donate, and invest green. Doing so is symbolically and actually significant. *Every dollar matters.*

INVEST IN THE ENVIRONMENT

Facts

- Investments can finance corporate environmental degradation *or* they can support positive corporate environmental practices.

- Socially Responsible Investing (SRI) is a financial strategy that focuses on both maximizing financial return on investments and on corporate practices that benefit the common social good.

- SRI is compatible with Christian values.

- SRI funds include socially and environmentally responsible corporations that produce safe and useful products using Earth-friendly practices while respecting human rights.

- Various SRI funds screen out companies involved in alcohol, tobacco, weapons, animal testing, human rights violations, and other products and practices inconsistent with social justice. Some funds specifically screen out environmentally unfriendly companies and invest in ones with green products and practices.

- Many of the largest mutual funds in the United States invest in companies with some of the worst global warming–causing corporate practices.

- More and more investors, including religious organizations, are choosing to invest in socially responsible funds.

Actions

- *Review* the church's current accounts to ascertain where monies are invested.

- *Research* the companies and funds for their policies and environmental records.

- *Be proactive* as an organization and as a shareholder:

  > Write letters to companies in which the church is invested inquiring about their environmental stewardship practices.

  > Use your status as a stockholder and part owner of a company to influence corporate decisions.

  > Let the company know your congregation wants environmentally friendly corporate behaviors.

- *Work with a financial advisor* who is knowledgeable about SRI.

+ *Vote* your proxies in favor of environmental protection action.

+ *Divest* from companies and funds who do not share your green values.

+ *Invest* in socially responsible mutual funds that share your green values.

Resources

+ *Compelling Returns: A Practical Guide to Socially Responsible Investing,* by S. J. Budde (Hobocken, N.J.: Wiley, 2008). This book provides an explanation of basic SRI strategies, ways to incorporate these strategies into investment portfolios, guidance on aligning investing with values, and a directory of SRI companies.

+ *The Complete Idiot's Guide to Socially Responsible Investing,* by Ken Little (New York: Alpha, 2008). This book provides information about the history and future of SRI, ways to evaluate the social responsibility commitment of companies, and performance comparisons between socially responsible investments and traditional investments.

+ Green America, 1612 K St. NW, Suite 600, Washington DC 20006; (800) 584-7336; *www.greenamericatoday.org/ socialinvesting.* This not-for-profit membership organization focuses on using economic power to create a socially just and sustainable society. Online and print education and social action materials are available including *The Financial Planning Handbook*, a guide to socially responsible investing, and the newsletter *Real Green*. A "Take Action" letter to mutual funds that invest in environmentally unfriendly companies is provided and can be signed online or used as a sample to write your own letters.

+ Green Money Journal, P.O. Box 67, Santa Fe, NM 87504; (505) 988-7423; *www.greenmoneyjournal.com.* This journal promotes awareness of socially and environmentally responsible business, investing, and consumer resources. The website publishes SRI-related articles and provides links to other online SRI resources.

- *Profitable Socially Responsible Investing: An Institutional Investor's Guide*, by Marc J. Lane (London: Institutional Investor Guides, 2005). This is an expensive resource for professional investors.

- Social Investment Forum, online at *www.socialinvest.org/ Areas/SRIGuide*. This national nonprofit membership organization promotes socially responsible investment practices. The website provides a guide to SRI, a list of and links to SRI financial consultants, and a list of mutual funds screened by their environmental record (and by other social issues such as alcohol, tobacco, weapons, defense, human rights, etc.).

- *Socially Responsible Investing: Making a Difference and Making Money*, by Amy Domini (Chicago: Dearborn Trade, 2001).

DONATE

Facts

- Over 80 percent of people in the United States donate to charities.

- In 2004 the average amount donated per person was over $1200.

- 65 percent of people give to a church or other place of worship (Barna Group 2005).

- Churches, in turn, donate to mission projects.

- Donating to environmental groups and projects can become part of your church's environmental stewardship practices.

Actions

- *Research* mission projects in the United States and around the world that focus on environmental concerns such as installation of solar panels or wind turbines, safe drinking water, or hunger.

- *Research* faith–environment education and action programs.

- *Research* environmental issues, groups, and projects in your local area.

- *Choose one or more* as recipients of church donations.

- *Make special donations* as part of your Earth Day celebration.

- *Donate* on a regular basis.

- *Establish partnership relationships* with local environmental groups and invite speakers from the groups to talk to your congregation.

Resources

- National Council of Churches Eco-Justice Programs; *www.nccecojustice.org*. Click on "Donate" to support their programs that provide faith–environment education and resources.

- Your denomination's mission programs.

- Local chapters of national environmental groups.

- Local grassroots environmental projects.

CREATE YOUR OWN CARBON OFFSETS FUND

Facts

- Church members who want to counterbalance their carbon emissions can purchase carbon offsets from vendors who build new clean energy projects to displace energy generated by burning fossil fuels.

 ◆ A church can establish its own carbon offset fund for installing clean energy systems.

Actions

 ◆ *Develop* a Church Carbon Offsets program.

 ◆ Provide instructions and assistance for members to *calculate their carbon emissions* (e.g., for their household for a month or year, for a trip by car or airplane).

 ◆ *Establish a special fund* for an identified green church project to generate clean, renewable energy. (Alternatively, you could fund other green projects that are not true carbon offsets — such as buying and installing low flush toilets, planting a garden, or purchasing compact florescent bulbs.)

 ◆ *Provide the opportunity for members to donate money* to offset all or a portion of their carbon emissions.

 ◆ As the fund grows, display a *graphic representation* of the amount of money needed for the project and the amount as it is donated.

 ◆ *Finance a renewable energy project* (or other green project) for the church.

Resources

 ◆ See "Become Carbon Neutral" (page 29 above) for further information and for links to carbon calculators.

Chapter Six

Children's Activities

Our children are an incredibly important component of the faith–
environment picture. They are affected more than adults by
mercury in the water, toxins in our cleaning products, chemicals on our lawns and food, and pollution in the air because of
three factors: Children are smaller than adults, and so the toxins to which they are exposed are proportionally greater in terms
of amount of toxin to body size. They are still in the process
of growing, and toxins potentially affect their neurological and
physical development. And they will be around longer to see the
consequences of human actions on the environment.

My generation has regrettably been responsible for the development of many products that have adversely affected our
planet, and it has stood by while the next generation of detrimental products and changes has emerged. In my lifetime I have
witnessed the glass-to-plastic and paper-to-plastic shift — plastic milk cartons, plastic ketchup bottles, plastic soda and juice
bottles, plastic bags and, well, plastic items too numerous to
mention. I have also seen the reusable-to-disposable shift — disposable pens, disposable razors, disposable electronic equipment,
disposable phones, disposable fast food containers, wrappers,
and utensils, and basically a rather comprehensively disposable
lifestyle. My generation, and the next, have embraced SUVs,
needlessly large homes, and consumerism. I believe it is now our

114

responsibility to turn around our bigger-brighter-louder-more-is-better lifestyle, and leave a legacy for our children that shows we value sustainable and meaningful lives.

It is often said that children are the future. True enough. And reason enough to be passionate environmental stewards. However, we are *all* the future. All the actions of all of us matter. My hope is that in all our decisions we learn to look more than a few months or years ahead, and that we learn to consider the effects of all our actions on the next generation, and on all the generations beyond the next one. My hope is that today's children learn at a young age to value the natural world, and that they take that value with them throughout their lives. My hope is that we teach our children well, that they live respectfully on the Earth — and that *they* teach *us* and motivate us to do the same.

Several activities that are intended to foster understanding and care of the Earth follow.

EARTH EGG

Description

This is an activity for older children (and adults) in which six participants represent the various "elements of the Earth." Together they balance an egg, which represents the Earth, to show the effects of human behavior on the interdependent web of creation.

An additional two people function as a Reader/facilitator and a Helper.

Purpose

- ◆ To demonstrate that:

  > all things are connected

  > human-caused environmental damage threatens the Earth

  > by changing our ways, we can save the Earth

Materials

* One egg (hard-boiled or not)

* 3 x 5 cards color-coded red and green

* Plain paper or cards

* Twelve lengths of heavy string or yarn cut into two-yard lengths

* One tube from a roll of toilet paper

* Six hats or caps

* Pictures, drawings, photos, stuffed animals, or other decorations for the hats

Directions

* Color or creatively decorate the egg to represent the Earth (you can use food coloring or cut a circle in a round piece of paper with a picture or drawing of the Earth on it, then fit it over the egg).

* Decorate one hat to represent each Earth Element:

Air	Rainforest
Animals	Soil
People	Water

* Copy the red card scenarios and the green card scenarios and glue them to the cards (see pages 119–121 for the scenarios).

* Make two card piles — one red and one green.

* Punch twelve evenly spaced holes in the tube about one inch from the top.

* Tie one string through each hole.

* Each of six Earth Element people put on a decorated hat

* The six Earth Elements hold one string in each hand.

- The Helper puts the egg on the tube so that it is balanced.

- Earth Elements keep the Earth Egg balanced and safe.

- The Helper draws one red card from the pile at random and reads it.

- The person holding the corresponding Earth Element drops one string — to indicate the negative effect of the action on that Element. Others redistribute themselves to keep the Earth Egg balanced.

- Another red card is drawn and read — and the corresponding Earth Element string is dropped. Again, others shift to maintain the balance of the Earth Egg.

- Another red card is drawn and read . . . and so on.

- Before the Earth Egg crashes and breaks, the Change Card is read aloud:

CHANGE CARD

The Earth Egg is about to be destroyed by human actions. Our actions can instead save it. We can save the Earth.

- Then the Reader draws and reads a green card.

- As positive change occurs as indicated on the green card, the Earth begins to be protected and restored. The Helper hands the corresponding dropped string to the Earth Element.

- Another green card is drawn and read, until the Earth Egg is again in perfect balance.

◆ Then the summary card is read by the Reader:

SUMMARY CARD

Everything in and on and of the Earth
is connected — the forests, soil, ocean,
rivers, lakes, air, animals, birds, farms, and
all the people throughout all the Earth.
What affects one thing, affects all things.
Our actions affect the Earth. We can
choose wise actions. We can protect
and restore the Earth to balance.

◆ All participants and those watching say a prayer of gratitude,
which can be written or projected for all to read:

PRAYER OF GRATITUDE

Thank you, God, for the gift of our beautiful Earth,
and for helping us to always be aware of the effects of our
*   actions.*
Thank you for all the Water, Air, Forests, and Soil,
and for all the Animals — human and otherwise.
Thank you for giving us the wisdom and courage to protect
*   the Earth*
and to act in ways that will bring us all into balance
*   once more.*

RED CARD SCENARIOS _____

Air: Coal is burned for electricity...and the AIR becomes polluted.

Air: Food is transported thousands of miles by trucks, ships, airplanes, so we can eat anything any time of year...and the AIR is polluted by burning transportation fuel.

Animals: Global warming melts the polar ice caps...and polar bears and other ANIMALS lose their homes.

Animals: We cut down forests to make paper...and birds and ANIMALS lose their homes.

People: As global warming causes climate change, more hurricanes, floods, and droughts occur...and PEOPLE are driven from their homes.

People: As industries pollute our water supplies...PEOPLE become sick and some even die.

Rainforest: We want palm oil to burn for energy...and so tropical RAINFORESTS are cut down to plant palms to supply fuel oil.

Rainforest: People drink lots of coffee...so farmers clear wide open spaces to grow lots of coffee as cheaply as possible...and so tropical RAINFORESTS are cut down to grow coffee.

Soil: Toxic chemicals are used as pesticides on food and other crops . . . and the SOIL is poisoned.

Soil: We grow one kind of crop on huge tracts of land with huge amounts of chemical fertilizers . . . until the SOIL has no life left in it and erodes away.

———————

Water: Toxic chemicals from old computers, TVs, printers, DVD players, and MP3s leach from landfills where they are thrown "away" . . . and pollute the ground WATER we drink.

Water: Coal, gas, and oil are burned to run cars, trucks, and airplanes, and to heat and light our homes. The pollution causes global warming . . . and the ocean WATER temperature rises.

GREEN CARD SCENARIOS _____

Air: We switch to clean energy from the sun, wind, and waves . . . and the AIR becomes clean.

Air: We walk, bike, vacation closer to home, and reduce our trips by cars and airplanes . . . and so the pollution caused by vehicles is reduced and the AIR becomes cleaner.

———————

Animals: We use less paper and recycle all the paper we do use . . . and trees are saved so ANIMALS and birds have a place to live.

Animals: We reduce our electricity and gasoline use . . . and global warming is reversed and the polar bears and other ANIMALS' homes are saved.

———————

People: We reduce our electricity and gasoline use... and global warming is reversed and PEOPLE are able to farm their land and feed themselves.

People: We let industries know we want them to make non-polluting, nontoxic products that can be completely recycled into new products. They "listen" and PEOPLE do not become sick from the pollution and the toxins.

_____

Rainforest: People switch to coffee grown in the shade of the forest... and RAINFORESTS are saved.

Rainforest: We switch to solar, wind, and wave power... and RAINFORESTS are left standing.

_____

Soil: We buy organically grown food and clothes made from organically grown cotton and other fibers... and the SOIL recovers to be clean and healthy.

Soil: We compost our kitchen and yard wastes and use it as fertilizer for our gardens... and so save landfill space and build healthy SOIL.

_____

Water: Electronic companies reduce the toxins in the products and recycle all the parts of old TVs, computers, printers, and MP3s... so they do not get dumped into a landfill, and the ground WATER becomes clean.

Water: We buy organically grown food and clothes made from organically grown cotton and other fibers... and the WATER is no longer polluted with pesticides, but becomes clean.

TOUCH THE HANDS
THAT TOUCH THE EARTH LIGHTLY

Description

This activity can be used during the Children's Church portion of a worship service or during an Earth Day celebration or other special event. After a brief introduction by an adult leader about the importance of caring for creation, the facilitator leads the group of children around the church to actually touch the hands of individuals who are stewards of the environment. As the children file past and touch a person's hand, the individual's specific environmental stewardship action is briefly described.

Purpose

◆ To recognize, honor, and bless individual members of the congregation whose actions demonstrate their environmental stewardship.

◆ To provide an opportunity for these stewards of the environment to serve as role models for the children and for others in the congregation.

Directions

◆ Talk with church members to learn who among you is actively engaged in environmental stewardship actions — small or large.

◆ Ask their permission to be included in this activity.

◆ Open with a few sentences about the importance of caring for God's creation.

◆ Lead the group of children around the sanctuary, if possible, to the people being recognized. Or alternatively, ask individuals to come forward.

- Say, "We touch the hands of those who touch the Earth lightly, and we ask God's blessing on them for what they do to protect and nurture our Earth."

- Lead the children past each person in turn. Have each child gently touch the hand of the first person being recognized as a brief description of the person's environmental stewardship activity is given. Then move on to the next environmental steward and do the same.

  Examples: "We touch the hand of Mr. Smith, who drives a car powered by biodiesel fuel from used restaurant grease"; "...of Beth, who rides her bike instead of driving a car to work; "...of Ann, who just installed a solar hot water heater at home"; "...of Betsy, who has an organic garden"; "...of Pastor Ron, who planted a shade tree in the church yard"; "...of Rosemary, who recently switched to drinking shade grown, organic coffee"; "...of Linda, who is a vegetarian"; "...of Bonnie, who organized our Fair Trade Fair"; "...of Rich, who carries reusable shopping bags to the store."

- After each person's hand has been touched and his or her action briefly described, have the children touch hands as a group, or hold hands in a circle, and say a prayer of thanksgiving and ask for blessings on these people and all people who "touch the Earth lightly."

PLANT A CHILDREN'S TREE

Description

This activity can be used during Sunday school, as part of an Earth Day celebration, as part of another special event, to honor someone, or to dedicate a new building or garden. A tree is planted in a location where it is easily accessible so the children of the church can be involved in its care, and where it can be used as a gathering place for Sunday school classes or other activities.

Purpose

- To involve children in a caring and nurturing nature activity.

- To help them learn about choosing, planting, caring for, and enjoying trees.

- To foster their personal investment in the church.

- To provide the benefits of the tree (e.g., beauty, shade, windbreak, fruit).

- To establish a place where children can meet for class or play.

Directions

- Determine the extent to which children and youth will be involved in the planning of the project, dependent on their age and ability.

- Link the planting to an occasion, dedication, memorial, or other event.

- Choose a location and a small tree.

- Have the children plant the tree (with assistance as needed).

- Install a permanent sign indicating it is "The Children's Tree."

- Gather around the tree as a congregation and bless it — possibly with everyone adding a scoop of water and symbolically committing to its care.

- Have children take responsibility for some of the tree care throughout the coming several years.

- Meet for children's Sunday school classes around the tree.

- Over the years, harvest fruit and nuts to eat or flowers and branches to use for decorations.

- Once the tree is large enough, hang a bird feeder to bring birds into the church yard and to symbolize abundance and sharing.

Chapter Seven

Special Projects

This chapter deals with an assortment of the topics that do not neatly fit better into one of the previous chapters. I have organized it into four categories: Publicity and Media, Events, Holidays, and Other.

The first category speaks to those ways a church communicates its green mission. Newsletters typically cover a lot of ground about church activities, and environmental stewardship activities are a nice addition. Increasing numbers of churches are wisely developing websites. They are now often the first contact point for a prospective member. Including information about your environmental stewardship beliefs and actions helps define your church for others, and might serve to attract like-minded people to your congregation.

Writing about the three themed events (zero waste, meat-free, and local foods) was one of my favorite parts of working on *Eco-Faith*. Any of the three events can be held separately — or a combination of any two or all three would work. The interesting, creative, and enjoyable possibilities of having one of these events are endless, and aspects of these events can become a regular part of other church activities. The concept of zero waste is certainly one to embrace wholeheartedly, though the idea of reducing meat consumption or going meat-free is a bit of a hard sell for many. A local foods event is ripe (both literally and figuratively) with possibilities. And considering the idea of a "carbon fast" (more accurately a carbon diet) during the Lenten season opens up many possibilities for education, study, and action. A zero waste Christmas is a great (though probably unfamiliar) idea. Embracing that concept, however, along with some of the other holiday suggestions, allows us to focus beyond some superficial traditions, and to create more meaningful and spiritual holidays.

Last, but absolutely not least, I address the church mission statement. Greening the mission statement is probably one of the easiest action steps to take, and maybe should be at the top of a church's greening agenda. Mission statements that truly reflect an organization's *reason for* being and *way of* being are vital. When created by a congregation in a thoughtful and concerted effort, a mission statement causes personal and organizational introspection and results in a clear and coherent declaration. For a congregation striving to be green, the mission statement should evolve into one that reflects the goal of environmental stewardship.

Publicity and Media _____

NEWSLETTERS

Facts

- Many congregations publish electronic or print newsletters.

- Adding a regular newsletter column focused on environmental issues at the local, world, congregational, and denominational levels is educational and can increase awareness and inspire action.

- Many denominations, faith-affiliated organizations, and environmental groups provide easily accessible information that can be incorporated into newsletter articles.

Actions

◆ *Start* a church newsletter and include an environment-focused column or add a "green" column to your existing newsletter.

◆ *Use the Resources section below and those found throughout this book* to locate online and print sources of relevant information to include in the newsletter.

Resources

◆ Earth Ministry, 6512 Twenty-third St., Suite 317, Seattle, WA 98117; (206) 632-2426; *www.earthministry.org*. This organization was founded in 1992 "to inspire and mobilize the Christian community to play a leadership role in building a just and sustainable future...[working] in partnership with congregations and individuals...for social change through environmental advocacy." Membership, programs, and resources are open to persons of all spiritual traditions. It is a good source of information for your newsletter.

◆ *Greening Congregations Handbook: Stories, Ideas, and Resources for Cultivating Creation Awareness and Care in Your Congregation,* edited by Tanya Marcovna Barnett (Seattle: Earth Ministry, 2002). This is a spiral-bound book of suggestions and resources from Earth Ministry.

◆ National Council of Churches Eco-Justice Programs, 110 Maryland Ave. NE, Suite 108, Washington, DC 20002; (202) 544-2350; *nccecojustice.org./about.html*. This program of the National Council of Churches of Christ facilitates and coordinates "national bodies of member Protestant and Orthodox denominations to work together to protect and restore God's Creation." The website provides information, education, an "Activist's Toolbox" of environmental steward-ship actions, links to multiple denominational and faith-based environmental resources, and online downloadable resources.

◆ National Religious Partnership for the Environment, 49 S. Pleasant St., Suite 301 Amherst, MA 01002; (413) 253-1515; *www.nrpe.org*. This is an association of independent faith groups including the U.S. Conference of Catholic Bishops, the National Council of Churches U.S.A., the Coalition on the Environment and Jewish Life, and the Evangelical Environmental Network. Partners draw upon their religious traditions for "scholarship, leadership training, congregation and agency initiatives, and public policy education in service to environmental sustainability and justice" and "to offer resources of religious life and moral vision to a universal effort to protect humankind's common home and well-being on Earth."

◆ *Saving God's Green Earth: Rediscovering the Church's Responsibility to Environmental Stewardship*, by Tri Robinson (Norcross, Ga.: Ampelon Publishing, 2006). This book was written by the founding pastor of the Vineyard Boise (Idaho) Church to encourage Christians to "embrace the biblical mandate to care for creation." A good source of information and inspiration for those writing newsletter articles.

◆ *Serve God, Save the Planet: A Christian Call to Action,* by J. Matthew Sleeth (White River Junction, Vt.: Chelsea Green Publishing, 2006). An interesting and enlightening book written by a physician about his journey from living the "American dream" lifestyle to drastically reducing his family's ecological footprint. He makes a clear and convincing case for Christians' responsibility in caring for the environment. Another good source of information and inspiration for those writing newsletter articles.

◆ Sierra Club, 85 Second St., 2nd Floor, San Francisco, CA 94105; (415)-977-5500; *www.sierraclub.org/partnerships/ faith/*. One of the Sierra Club's Environmental Partnerships programs is "Faith and the Environment." The website provides links to articles about faith-based environmental activities, Earth Day resources for communities of faith, summaries of and links to actions churches are initiating, partnership actions between the Sierra Club and faith groups, and links to multiple faith and environment websites.

WEBSITES

Facts

- Over 220 million people use the Internet in the United States.

- The percentage of the U.S. population that accesses the Internet grows each year.

- From 2000 to 2008 the percentage increased from 41 percent of the population to over 72 percent.

- Your website is likely to be the initial contact of someone who is looking for a church.

- Making your church's green values, mission, and projects prominent on the website might set your congregation apart from others and serve to attract people interested in environmental stewardship.

—Statistics from Internet World Stats. See Resources.

Actions

- *Develop* a church website and include a section on your church's environmental stewardship actions or add an environmental stewardship section to your existing website.

- *Create a green logo* specific to your church, and use it prominently on the website.

- *Post the green column* from the church newsletter.

- *Include links* to other relevant websites that combine information about religious faith and environmental stewardship.

- *Showcase articles and photos* of the church environmental activities.

Resources

- Internet World Stats: Usage and Population Statistics; *www.internetworldstats.com/am/us.htm*. This website provides statistics on U.S. Internet usage, and was the source for the "Facts" section statistics above.

- Relevant links to choose from to post on the environment and faith page of your church website:

  > *www.christianaid.org.uk/stoppoverty/climatechange/index .aspx,* Christian Aid, Stop Poverty, Climate Change.

  > *www.homelandministries.org/PublicWitness/environment .htm,* Christian Church (Disciples of Christ), Eco-justice/ environmental ministries.

  > *www.webofcreation.org/Earthbible/earthbible.html;* Earth Bible: Reading the Bible from the Perspective of the Earth.

  > *eenonline.org/,* The Episcopal Ecological Network.

  > *www.creationcare.org/,* Evangelical Environmental Network and *Creation Care* magazine.

  > *environment.harvard.edu/religion/main.html,* The Forum on Religion and Ecology.

  > *www.revision.org,* National Association of Evangelicals, Re:Vision, Protecting Creation.

  > *nccecojustice.org./about.html,* National Council of Churches Eco-Justice Programs.

> *www.nrpe.org/*, The National Religious Partnership for the Environment.

> *www.pcusa.org/environment/*, Presbyterian Church USA Environmental Justice Ministries.

> *www.prcweb.org/*, Presbyterians for Restoring Creation.

> *www.theregenerationproject.org/*, The Regeneration Project and the Interfaith Power and Light campaign.

> *www.sierraclub.org/partnerships/faith*, Sierra Club, Faith and the Environment.

> *www.tearfund.org/Campaigning*, Tearfund, a United Kingdom–based Christian relief and development agency.

> *www.ucc.org/earthcare*, United Church of Christ, EarthCare.

> *www.uuministryforearth.org/cgi/news.cgi*, Unitarian Universalist Ministry for Earth.

> *www.usccb.org/sdwp/ejp/climate/index.shtml*, U.S. Conference of Catholic Bishops. Climate Change, Justice, and Health Initiative.

> *www.energystar.gov/index.cfm?c=small_business.sb_ congregations*, U.S. Environmental Protection Agency, Energy Star Congregations.

CREATE A GREEN RESOURCE LIBRARY
Facts

◆ Education about environmental issues alone is not enough to bring about behavior change, but it is a necessary component.

◆ A church-based library of books, movies, magazines, journals, and other resources provides church members free and easy access to materials on environmental and religious faith issues.

Actions

◆ *Designate a shelf or area in the church office* as the "Creation Care," "Theology-Ecology," or "Green" section.

◆ *Acquire* related periodicals, books, denominational literature, DVDs/videos. Purchase resources and accept donations of resources.

◆ *Publicize* the available resources on the church website or in the bulletin.

◆ *Loan* these resources to interested parties.

Resources

◆ *E: The Environmental Magazine* is available by subscription from Subscription Department, P.O. Box 2047, Marion, OH 43306-2147. This magazine is chock full of information, articles, products, and resources.

◆ Green America, 1612 K St. NW, Suite 600, Washington, DC 20006; (800) 584-7336; *www.greenamericatoday.org*. Joining this not-for-profit organization will provide the resource library with publications including the *National Green Pages* (a directory of screened green businesses), *Green American* (a quarterly publication with an in-depth focus on a specific social/economic justice topic), *Real Green* (a green financial newsletter) and the *Financial Planning Handbook* (a guide to socially responsible investing).

◆ *The Green Bible: New Revised Standard Version* (San Francisco: HarperOne, 2008). This Bible highlights the scriptures that relate to creation care. It also includes essays and resources.

◆ Include books about native plants specific to your geographical region.

◆ Find books and other materials for your resource library throughout *Eco-Faith*. Check the Resources sections as well as the Recommended Readings lists beginning on page 197.

◆ *Films* worth acquiring:

> *The 11th Hour.* A sobering but hopeful 2007 film produced and narrated by Leonardo DiCaprio that examines the climate crisis and the solutions; available on DVD at *www.11thhourfilm.com*

> *An Inconvenient Truth.* The 2006 documentary film of Al Gore's "traveling global warming show"; available on DVD at *www.climatecrisis.net*

> *Kilowatt Ours: A Plan to Re-energize America,* by Jeff Barrie. A film about America's energy problems and solutions that challenges people to conserve energy, use renewable energy, and create a "net zero nation"; available at *www.kilowattours.org*

> *Lighten Up! A Religious Response to Global Warming.* A twenty-minute film in which the president of the Regeneration Project, Rev. Canon Sally Bingham, speaks on global warming and environmental stewardship for congregations. DVD and VHS versions are available from the Regeneration Project website for a donation. From the homepage *www.theregenerationproject.org* click on "Resources."

> *Planet Earth.* An eleven-part BBC series released in 2007 with gorgeous nature footage and a message regarding the need for conservation efforts. Each fifty-minute episode features a specific geographical region or a specific type of wildlife habitat. Sir David Attenborough narrates.

Events _____

HOLD A ZERO WASTE EVENT

Facts

* Most consumer products are considered to be disposable — used briefly (a few minutes or a few years) and then discarded.

* We say we throw things "away," but there is really no "away."

* Plastics and polystyrene foam do not biodegrade and never really go "away."

* Trash in the landfill is not "away," it is in the landfill.

* Landfills, incinerators, and other waste treatment facilities are disproportionately located in neighborhoods of poor people and people of color. This phenomenon is known as "environmental racism." (See *Toxic Wastes and Race at Twenty* in Resources.)

* Waste treatment facilities release toxic chemicals, pollute water, air, and soil, and cause severe health problems for those living nearby.

* "Zero waste" is the concept of creating no waste.

* Nature recycles everything back to nature. It is the closed-loop, zero-waste, *natural cycle.*

* Industry does not, but could, recycle everything back through a closed-loop, zero-waste, *technological cycle.*

* Extended producer responsibility (EPR), a concept originating in Europe, holds manufacturers financially and physically responsible for the entire life cycle of their consumer products and packaging (Imhoff, 2005) — providing a strong incentive for them to create a circular system in which what was once considered *waste* is instead designed to be a *resource* for new products.

- We can have a voice at the industry level by using our purchasing power and by directly contacting manufacturers and legislators.

- Zero waste at the individual level means creating our own closed-loop, circular system — much like nature.

- We can do this in our homes.

- Church events can become zero waste events.

Actions

- Buy products with no packaging or the *least packaging* possible; use your *purchasing power voice.*

- *Write letters to manufacturers* voicing concerns about overpackaging and about waste generated by their products.

- *Designate and publicize* a church dinner, movie night, meeting, conference, or other event as a zero waste event.

- *Send invitations, agendas, and information by email,* and telephone those who are not connected electronically.

- *Serve food whose scraps can be composted* in the compost pile or bin.

- *Serve locally produced food* and beverages to decrease transportation-related carbon emissions.

- *Serve water in pitchers,* not plastic bottles.

- *Recycle* glass, steel, and aluminum containers; these are all truly recyclable.

- Use dinnerware and utensils that can be *washed and reused.*

- Consider asking participants to *bring their own reusable* dinnerware.

- *Use compostable, biodegradable dinnerware* and utensils if you have a way to compost them.

◆ *Use compostable, biodegradable "biobags"* instead of petroleum based plastic bags.

◆ *Minimize the need for paper* by posting the agenda or other information online or on a notice board at church.

◆ *Use natural decorations.*

◆ Give any awards, prizes, and gifts *without any wrapping paper,* or wrap in reusable fabric bags, old calendars or newspapers, or in natural fabric towels or napkins.

◆ Make all choices and decisions for the event with an eye to *closing the loop.*

◆ Estimate and calculate any greenhouse gas emissions generated by the event, and *purchase carbon offsets or contribute to the church's own carbon offset fund.*

◆ *Make zero waste your goal* for every church event.

Resources

◆ *Cradle to Cradle: Remaking the Way We Make Things,* by W. McDonough and M. Braungart (New York: North Point Press, 2002). This book is written by a chemist and an architect who are proponents of design processes that ensure that waste is not generated; natural products return to the cycle of nature and become "biological nutrients," and technology products return to the industrial cycle and become "technical nutrients."

◆ Eco-Cycle, P.O. Box 19006, Boulder, CO 80308; 5030 Pearl St., Boulder, CO 80301; (303) 444-6634; *www.ecocycle.org.* This county-based organization provides information and resources for its local area, though much of the information (e.g., about recycling, composting, buying recycled products) can be useful to others. Click on "Zero Waste" and "Zero Waste Event Kit" (available for purchase, but must be picked

up there). View the video on the website, or purchase it in
DVD or CD format.

♦ *Getting to Zero Waste* (*Co-op America Quarterly,* no. 73,
2007). Available on the website to read, or print as a PDF file.
You can order a hard copy at *www.greenamericatoday.org/
pubs/caq*. This is an excellent resource with articles about the
waste stream, environmental racism, the three Rs, "cradle to
cradle" design, and electronic waste.

♦ *Paper or Plastic: Searching for Solutions to an Overpackaged
World,* by Daniel Imhoff (San Francisco: Sierra Club Books,
2005). This thought-provoking book details the significant and
avoidable negative environmental effects of overpackaging,
and provides solutions across the whole product spectrum
from the manufacturers to the consumers.

♦ *Toxic Wastes and Race at Twenty, 1987–2007: A Report
Prepared for the United Church of Christ Justice and Witness Ministries,* by R. D. Bullard, P. Mohai, R. Saha, and
B. Wright (United Church of Christ, 2007); (800) 537-3396;
www.ucc.org/justice/environmental-racism. This is a follow-up
to the 1987 report that identified "environmental racism" and
coined the term. The earlier study found that the location
of toxic waste facilities was directly correlated with poverty
and with neighborhoods of people of color. The 2007 study
found the same thing and determined that race was the factor
most predictive of where toxic waste facilities are located. The
165-page report can be viewed on the website or downloaded.
Print copies of both reports are available at no cost except
shipping and handling.

♦ Zero Waste Alliance, One World Trade Center, 121 SW
Salmon St., Suite 210 Portland, OR 97204; (503) 279-9383;
www.zerowaste.org. This is a nonprofit organization that
works with universities, government agencies, and businesses

to promote the use of zero waste strategies. It helps businesses and organizations reduce or eliminate waste and toxins and to become more "efficient, competitive, profitable, and environmentally responsible." The website provides basic zero waste information and helpful graphics.

HOLD A MEAT-FREE EVENT

Facts

* One of the most "inconvenient truths" for many of us is that meat eating is a major contributor to environmental problems.

* The average meat consumption in industrialized countries is about 187 pounds per person per year compared to about 70 pounds in developing countries.

* And at least 60 percent of meat is produced in developing countries (Nierenberg 2008).

* Before the 1960s and the advent of factory farms, livestock was raised on family farms without "antibiotics, added hormones, feed additives, flavor enhancers, age-delaying gases and saltwater solutions" (Robinson 2008).

* Health concerns arise related to growth hormones, antibiotics, "mad cow disease," and E. coli.

* Factory-farm-raised cattle on feedlots, or animal feeding operations (AFO), are fed high-grain diets (along with low quality junk feed) to induce unnaturally rapid rates of growth. This leads to sickness in the animals and treatment with and preventive use of antibiotics.

* According to a 2006 United Nations report, *livestock is one of the main sources of global warming greenhouse gases*. The report, *Livestock's Long Shadow* (United Nations 2006), says: "Climate change is the most serious challenge facing the human race. The livestock sector is a major player, responsible

for 18 percent of greenhouse gas emissions measured in CO_2 equivalent."

> Of human-related emissions, livestock is responsible for 9 percent of CO_2 emissions, 37 percent of methane, 65 percent of nitrous oxide, and 64 percent of ammonia.

> Livestock use 70 percent of all agricultural land.

> Livestock (and their feed crops) use 30 percent of the world's land surface.

> This land was once wildlife habitat and so "most of the world's threatened species are suffering habitat loss where livestock are a factor."

> 70 percent of former Amazon forest land is now used for grazing.

> In the United States, livestock are responsible for 37 percent of pesticide use and 50 percent of antibiotic use.

> Livestock-related activities lead to deforestation, reduction in biodiversity, land degradation (overgrazing, soil compaction, erosion), and water pollution (from wastes, hormones, antibiotics, pesticides, and fertilizers).

• The EPA and Department of Agriculture also report a multitude of negative environmental impacts related to livestock farming.

• According to *Vegetarian Times,* approximately 70 percent of all U.S. grain is fed to animals raised for slaughter, and U.S. livestock consume five times more grain than U.S. humans.

• Meat eating is an inefficient use of water and fossil fuels and causes way more GHG emissions and other pollution than does plant eating.

- Plant eating is efficient; it is not feeding food to food (as is raising plants, feeding them to animals, then feeding the animals to people).

- Meat consumption continues to increase around the world.

- Seafood caught in unsustainable ways or raised in fish farms that cause water pollution and destroy wetlands is also a source of environmental problems.

- According to the American Dietetic Association (2003), a good vegetarian diet is healthful, nutritionally sound, and provides health benefits.

- However, vegetables, fruits, and grains grown with the use of heavy pesticide and fertilizer applications or transported long distances to provide consumers with out-of-season produce are also environmentally unfriendly.

- Reducing meat consumption, like reducing energy use, can reduce our "footprint" on the Earth.

- We all have to eat, and we can make informed choices to lessen the negative environmental impacts.

- Holding a meat-free church dinner can raise awareness of the relationship between our food and our Earth, and possibly result in people choosing to reduce their overall meat consumption.

- By reducing meat consumption, we reduce our carbon footprint on the Earth.

Actions

- *Research* available food, faith, and environment resources.

- *Provide information* about the effects of our food choices on the Earth and on the people of the Earth related to:

> energy use

> pollution

> deforestation and desertification

> habitat loss

> loss of biodiversity

> hunger

> health

● *Plan* a meat-free church event.

● *Determine any other menu criteria:*

> animal product–free (i.e., no dairy or eggs)

> seasonal

> locally grown

> organic

● *Announce and promote* the event via your bulletin, newsletter, and website.

● Consider soliciting *media coverage.*

● Use food and faith resources to graphically or actually *demonstrate the differences* between a typical American meal and a typical meal in a poor country.

● *Make meat-free or reduced meat consumption your goal* for some church events.

● *Enjoy* healthy, nutritious, and beautiful food at the event!

Resources

● *Animal, Vegetable, Miracle: A Year of Food Life,* by Barbara Kingsolver, with Steven L. Hopp and Camille Kingsolver (New York: HarperCollins, 2007). This well-known author, her husband, and her daughter write of the family's year of eating home-grown, locally produced, and home-preserved foods.

◆ Eat Well Guide, *www.eatwellguide.org/i.php?pd=Home*. This is a source of local, sustainable, and organic restaurants, co-ops, and stores in the United States and Canada by zip or postal code.

◆ *The Food Revolution: How Your Diet Can Help Save Your Life and Our World,* by John Robbins (Berkeley, Calif.: Conari Press, 2001).

◆ *Hope's Edge: The Next Diet for a Small Planet,* by Frances Moore Lappé and Anna Lappé (New York: Tarcher, 2003). This book is by the author of the 1972 classic *Diet for a Small Planet.*

◆ Local Harvest, *www.localharvest.org.* This website is a source for locating online stores, grocery stores, farms, co-ops, restaurants, CSAs (community supported agriculture programs), and other sources of "real food."

◆ Natural Resources Defense Council (NRDC), *www.nrdc.org.* Type "meat consumption" into "Search" for related articles such as "Another Reason to Eat Less Meat" and "Pollution from Giant Livestock Farms Threatens Public Health."

◆ North American Vegetarian Society (NAVS), online at *www.navs-online.org.* This nonprofit organization promotes a vegetarian lifestyle and sponsors an annual World Vegetarian Day on October 1. Go to *www.worldvegetarianday.org.* The website is friendly to nonvegetarians and encourages them to have a meat-free meal, or to eat meat-free for a day or a month. Very inexpensive educational materials that could be used for your meat-free event are available.

◆ *The Omnivore's Dilemma: A Natural History of Four Meals,* by Michael Pollan (New York: Penguin, 2007). The author discusses the food (and meals) produced from industrial farms, big business, and smaller organic farms, as well as the food he hunted or gathered himself.

- Presbyterian Church USA, Hunger Program, *www.pcusa.org/hunger/index.htm*. Click on the "Food and Faith" icon for articles, actions ideas, and resources, and *Just Eating? Practicing Our Faith at the Table,* a seven-week curriculum for congregations.

- Sierra Club, *www.sierraclub.org*. Click on "Our Conservation Initiatives," "More Programs," then under "More Environmental Issues," click on "Factory Farms."

- Sustainable Table, *www.sustainabletable.org*. This online resource related to food sustainability features an abundance of information on food issues and actions and very nice downloadable brochures, fact sheets, handouts, and even a movie.

- UN News Centre, "Rearing Cattle Produces More Greenhouse Gases Than Driving Cars, UN Report Warns." To read this article about the 2006 United Nations report, see online *www.un.org/apps/news/story.asp?NewsID=20772&Cr=global&Cr1=warming*. For a summary of the report, *Livestock's Long Shadow,* and access to the entire report see online *www.virtualcentre.org/en/library/key_pub/longshad/A0701E00.htm*

- U.S. Department of Agriculture and U.S. Environmental Protection Agency. To access the March 1999 joint report by these two agencies, "Unified National Strategy for Animal Feeding Operations" go to *www.epa.gov/npdes/pubs/finafost.pdf*.

- *Vegetarian Times* magazine, *www.vegetariantimes.com*. This magazine and website is devoted to vegetarianism and is a good source for recipes and nutrition information. Click on "Resources," then "Why Go Veg?" for a list of reasons to eat meat-free.

- Worldwatch Institute; Vital Signs Online; *www.worldwatch .org/vsonline*. This useful tool provides information and analysis about global trends. For statistics and trends related to the topic at hand, click on "Meat Production," "Fish," and "Egg Production." The site also covers many other topics.

HOLD A LOCAL FOODS EVENT

Facts

- Another "inconvenient truth" related to our food is that much of it travels great distances — and so contributes significantly to global warming through the burning of fossil fuels for transporting it.

- A growing trend is to eat locally — often defined as within a hundred-mile radius.

- The newly coined word for a person who eats locally is "locavore." "Locavore" was the Oxford American Dictionary's 2007 Word of the Year.

- Buying local supports local businesses — often small, family owned, and sustainably operated ones.

- We can make informed choices to lessen the negative environmental impacts by eating less food from afar and more locally produced food.

- Holding a church dinner of local foods can raise awareness of the relationship between our food and our Earth. It may result in people choosing to reduce their consumption of food that has traveled thousands of miles, and increase consumption of local foods.

- By reducing consumption of distant foods, we decrease our carbon footprint.

Actions

- *Research* available food, faith, and environment resources.

- *Provide information* about the effects of our food choices on the Earth and on the people of the Earth related to the environmental, economic, and social costs.

- Have *education materials* (e.g., books, posters, brochures) available for interested people prior to and at the event.

- Have local foods as a *topic for an adult study class.*

- *Plan* a local foods church dinner or other event.

- *Determine the criteria* for food on the menu — specifically what distance or other criteria (e.g., within your state) defines "local" for your event.

- *Buy food* from farmer's markets, community supported agriculture (CSA) programs, local family farms, bakeries, cheese makers, bee keepers, and orchards — and from *home gardeners and hunters* in your midst. If you grow edibles on church grounds, by all means include those.

- *Determine the format* for the event — shared food preparation or "potluck."

- *Announce and promote* the event via your bulletin, newsletter, and website.

- Consider soliciting *media coverage* for your environmentally responsible, educational, and creative event.

- *Make increased use of local products your goal* for other church events.

- *Enjoy* nutritional and beautiful local food at the event!

Resources

- *Animal, Vegetable, Miracle: A Year of Food Life,* by Barbara Kingsolver, with Steven L. Hopp and Camille Kingsolver (New York: HarperCollins, 2007). This well-known author, her husband, and her daughter write of the family's year of eating home-grown, locally produced, and home-preserved foods.

- Eat Well Guide, *www.eatwellguide.org/i.php?pd=Home.* This is a source of local, sustainable, and organic restaurants, co-ops, and stores in the United States and Canada by zip or postal code.

- Local Harvest, *www.localharvest.org.* This website is a source for locating online stores, grocery stores, farms, co-ops, restaurants, CSAs, and other sources of "real food."

- Locavores, *locavores.com.* This San Francisco–based group promotes and educates about eating local.

- *Plenty: One Man, One Woman, and a Raucous Year of Eating Locally,* by Alisa Smith and J. B. MacKinnon (New York: Harmony, 2007). This couple writes of their experiences of eating only food grown within a hundred miles of their British Columbia home. The Canadian edition of the book is titled *The 100-Mile Diet: A Year of Local Eating.* Visit their website at *www.100milediet.org.*

- Presbyterian Church USA, Hunger Program, *www.pcusa.org/hunger/index.htm.* Click on the "Food and Faith" icon for articles, action ideas, and resources, and *Just Eating? Practicing our Faith at the Table* — a seven-week curriculum for congregations.

- Sustainable Table; *www.sustainabletable.org.* This online resource related to food sustainability features an abundance of information on food issues and actions, and downloadable brochures, fact sheets, handouts, and even a movie.

Holidays _____

FAST FROM CARBON FOR LENT

Facts

- Lent is the forty-day pre-Easter Christian season of prayer and fasting symbolic of the time Jesus spent alone in the wilderness where he fasted and resisted temptation by the devil (Matt. 4:1–2; Mark 1:12–13; Luke 4:1–3).

- Fasting or giving up specific foods or activities for Lent has been a common practice for Christians from ancient times to the present.

- Instead of just fasting from food or festivities, you can choose to take an action on each of the forty days of Lent that will have much farther reaching effects: go on a "carbon fast."

- Climate change affects everyone — and the poor of the world are especially negatively affected.

- English Bishop James Jones councils us to "fast" from carbon for Lent "to help the poor of the world."

- Richer and industrialized countries emit the most carbon per person, poor countries the least. Bishop Jones stated, "It is an offence to God to treat people unjustly — and our carbon emissions are just that: unjust" (Tearfund 2008).

- Decreasing energy use can be accomplished in many ways.

Actions

- *Plan a "Carbon Fast" at your church* to occur during the Lenten season.

- *Build a Lenten worship service* around the topic of the negative effects of the climate crisis on the very people that the church is otherwise helping through mission work.

- *Focus* the service and church activities on environmental stewardship as a necessary component of Christian mission work.

- *Make a list* of forty carbon emission–reducing actions (or use the Tearfund list — see Resources).

- *Choose* one of the forty actions and do it everyday, or choose a different action on each of the forty days. Do this as individuals or as a congregation.

- *Offer a one-to-four-week adult study* or Sunday school class on the climate crisis and the reasons to embark on a carbon fast as a faith community.

- *Reflect* on the reasons you are "fasting" from carbon each time you turn off a light, change to a CFL bulb, walk instead of driving, take your groceries home in a reusable bag instead of plastic, or drink tap water instead of water bottled in plastic.

Resources

- Tearfund, 100 Church Rd., Teddington, TW11 8QE, *www.tearfund.org/Churches/Carbon+fast+new;* or search "carbon fast" in "all tearfund" from the home page. Tearfund is a Christian relief and development agency based in England that works with local churches worldwide "to help eradicate poverty." The website offers resources for your church to plan and participate in a carbon fast including sermon notes, study guides, PowerPoint presentations, a sample list of forty carbon emission–reducing actions (which can be adapted for use in the United States), and information about the relevance of environmental stewardship to Christians.

I'M DREAMING OF A GREEN CHRISTMAS

Facts

- Christmas holidays for many have turned into times of *excess* — excessive buying, eating, drinking, stress, packaging, wrapping, and waste.

- According to the California Integrated Waste Management Board:

  > An *extra* million tons of waste is generated each week in the United States between Thanksgiving and Christmas.

  > Tens of thousands of miles of ribbon are discarded each year — more than enough to tie around the Earth.

- Increased pollution is generated by extra and often excessive use of electricity for lighting, decorations, cooking, and driving.

- Increased paper use (for wrapping and cards) means more trees are cut down, more air and water is polluted, and more toxic waste is generated in the manufacturing process.

- As people of faith, we can do better — both spiritually and ecologically.

Actions

- *Create a focus on greening the holidays* through related sermons, prayers, newsletter articles, and Advent activities.

- As a congregation and individuals, *be conscious consumers:* consider what you buy, where it came from, and its current and future impact on the planet.

- Decorate the sanctuary with *greens* and with fewer or no extra lights.

- Decorate the Christmas tree without using strings of lights, or use *LED lights* (which use 90 percent less electricity than like-sized incandescent bulbs).

- Have a *preholiday fair trade fundraiser* selling coffee, tea, cocoa, olive oil, vanilla, candy, and handicrafts.

- Switch from petroleum-based *candles* to ones made of beeswax, soy, or other vegetable wax.

- *Recycle Christmas trees* for mulch.

- To green their personal holidays, *encourage members to:*

  > Give handmade gifts.

  > Help children make gifts.

  > Buy locally made items.

  > Avoid excessively packaged items.

  > Give gift certificates for their time, energy, and talents.

  > Give tickets to a play, concert, or movie.

  > Give gifts that are durable and will be long-lasting.

  > Take canvas or other reusable bags to the store when you shop; avoid plastic bags.

  > Send tree-free paper cards, or ones made of 100 percent recycled paper, preferably printed with soy or other vegetable-based ink.

  > Wrap gifts in recycled materials such as old maps, newspaper comics, wallpaper samples, old sheet music, and out-of-date calendar photos.

  > Wrap gifts in cloth napkins, kitchen towels, or handkerchiefs so the wrapping becomes part of the present.

  > Wrap and tie packages with reusable ribbon, fabric, raffia, or yarn.

> Make cloth gift bags and reuse them year after year for decades.

> Use flowers, pine-cones, greens, herbs, or other natural package decorations.

> Pack gifts to be mailed using real popcorn or biodegradable corn starch packing material instead of polystyrene "peanuts."

> Give solar-powered radios, flashlights, and cell phone chargers.

> Make gift tags from last year's cards.

> Give memberships or donations to local, national, or global social and Earth justice organizations.

> Decrease holiday waste, stress, and spending.

> Increase:

  - time spent with family and friends

  - gifts of energy, time, and talent

  - volunteer work

  - donations

  - singing

  - praying

  - thoughtfulness

  - compassion

  - loving kindness

  - Earth-friendly practice

Resources

- California Integrated Waste Management Board; 1001 I St., P.O. Box 4025, Sacramento, CA 95812-4025; (916) 341-6300; *www.ciwmb.ca.gov.* This is the state agency that oversees, manages, and tracks California's 92 million tons of waste generated each year. Find holiday waste reduction tips at *www.ciwmb.ca.gov/PublicEd/Holidays.*

- Center for a New American Dream, 6930 Carroll Ave., Suite 900, Takoma Park, MD 20912; (301) 891-3683 or (877) 68-DREAM; *www.newdream.org/holiday.* "Simplify the Holidays" offers holiday tips and resources, creative and eco-friendly gift ideas, tips on organizing an alternative gift fair, printable "Gift of Time" cards, and a free downloadable brochure. Their motto is "More Fun, Less Stuff!"

- *The Consumer's Guide to Effective Environmental Choices: Practical Advice from the Union of Concerned Scientists,* by Michael Brower and Warren Leon (New York: Three Rivers Press, 1999). This practical guidebook of information helps consumers set priorities regarding their purchasing actions based on analyses of the relative negative impact of various consumer decisions.

- Environmental Defense Fund, 257 Park Ave. South, New York, NY 10010; (800) 684-3322; *www2.edf.org/home.cfm.* This website provides many suggestions for greening the holidays. Search "holidays" from the home page.

- Reduce.org, *www.reduce.org.* This is a resource-packed website of the Minnesota Pollution Control Agency. Click on "At the Holidays" for environmentally friendly holiday ideas.

- *Shopping with a Conscience,* by Duncan Clark and Richie Unterberger (New York: Rough Guides, 2007). This book offers useful information for consumers who want to learn how to align their purchases with their values.

- Treehugger, *www.treehugger.com*. This website aims to be a "one-stop shop for green news, solutions, and product information." Under "Take Action," click on "Green Gift Guide."

- Use Less Stuff, *www.use-less-stuff.com/ulsday/42ways.html*. This website provides a checklist of "simple things you can do to reduce waste while you eat, drink, and make merry this holiday season."

- U.S. Environmental Protection Agency (EPA), Office of Solid Waste (5305P), 1200 Pennsylvania Ave. NW, Washington, DC 20460; *www.epa.gov/epaoswer/osw/specials/funfacts/winter.htm*. This EPA website offers tips for "Reducing Holiday Waste."

- Washington Department of Natural Resources and Parks, Solid Waste Division, King St. Center, 201 S. Jackson St., Suite 701, Seattle, Washington 98104; (206) 296-4466; (800) 325-6165 ext. 66542. See their discount offers for "experience gifts" for Seattle-area activities at *www.metrokc.gov/dnrp/swd/wastefreeholidays*.

Other _____

UPDATE YOUR MISSION STATEMENT

Facts

- A mission statement is a short summary of your church's purpose, goals, and philosophies.

- It succinctly describes the core principles and intentions of the members of the church.

- A church with a commitment to environmental stewardship should make that evident in its mission statement.

Actions

- *Review* the current mission statement.

- *Evaluate* it for comprehensiveness (i.e., does it include environmental stewardship?).

- *Solicit suggestions* from members of the congregation on how best to incorporate the church's commitment to environmental stewardship.

- *Write or rewrite the mission statement* to include the church's green mission.

- *Consider including words or phrases* such as "Earth care," "environmental stewardship," "Earth justice," "eco-faith," "care of creation," "celebrate, restore, and nurture the Earth," "eco-justice" or "to live in harmony with all of God's creation."

Resources

- *Greening Congregations Handbook: Stories, Ideas, and Resources for Cultivating Creation Awareness and Care in Your Congregation,* edited by Tanya Marcovna Barnett (Seattle: Earth Ministry, 2002). This spiral-bound book of suggestions and resources from Earth Ministry offers information on green mission statements (see section 3, pages 5–6).

- *MissionStatements.com* is a website collection of various mission statements that can serve as examples for writing your own. It has a section on church mission statements at *www.missionstatements.com/church_mission_statements .html.* None are specifically focused on the interconnection between religion and the environment, but they might inspire some creative thought for your own church's statement.

PART TWO

Inspiring Stories from around the Country

The following are but a few of the many stories of congregations from across the United States who are going green. And of these few, my accounts tell only a part of their larger stories. I was fortunate enough to have a good excuse to track down these stories. I was looking for "inspiring" examples of environmental stewardship for this book. That was my entrée to many interesting people and many interesting stories.

By email and telephone I communicated with ministers, office administrators, a program administrator, a priest, a director of fundraising, and others — some of the most dedicated and enthusiastic environmental stewards you can imagine. For only one of the stories did I gather information in-person and on-site since I live in Hawai'i, far from places like Michigan and Rhode Island, and, well, actually far from everyplace else. In fact Hawai'i is one of the most geographically remote places on the planet (second only to Easter Island in distance from a large land mass). So time, money, and carbon footprint considerations precluded my visiting all the people and places you will read about. However, in addition to Hawai'i's visual beauty and great weather, living here provided me with the opportunity to visit Kawaiaha'o Church School in Honolulu and see firsthand their Earth-friendly actions with the young students. The importance of starting children on a green path early on cannot be overstated, and they do a great job of this at Kawaiaha'o. You will read about what I found there, as well as about greening a rectory in Michigan, restoring an area with native plants in Maryland, holding a climate action rally on the beach in Rhode Island, and eliminating trash from post-worship lunches in the nation's capitol. In addition you will read the remarkable story of the Friends Center in the heart of Philadelphia becoming a very deep shade of green.

When I finished my writing, I noticed that much of *Eco-Faith* has something to do with water. Many of the inspiring stories also have a water connection. From the freshwater spring at Kawaiaha'o School, to providing clean water to people in Africa, preventing storm water runoff and water pollution, opposing privatization of aquifers and the bottling and selling of water out from under local people, or holding a rally to bring attention to the global-warming-related plight of the shoreline and marine life, water is prominent in the picture. When I talk about water or the ocean throughout the book, I generally do not refer to it in the plural (e.g., waters or oceans). Though the plural seems more poetic, I often use the singular because I want us to begin thinking of the *connection* of all water on the planet. It is an interconnected flow that includes the water of the ocean worldwide, the water of the polar ice caps, the water of the rain, the water of our bodies. The water is all connected. Being aware of this connectedness facilitates our *commitment* and *action*.

Be inspired. Do not be wary of the road ahead. The only real thing to be afraid of is the consequences of inaction. You don't need to know everything before you take the plunge to begin greening your congregation or take on your next green project.

You don't need to have every single person on board. People with little or no interest, and even the naysayers, will come around once they truly understand the issues, the connections, and the (negative and positive) consequences of all of our behaviors. We are responsible for caring for all the holy lands, all the sacred water, and all the inhabitants of God's creation. All of them. At home, at work, at our place of worship, and with every step we take.

Read the stories. Be inspired. Take action.
Every action matters.

URBAN GREEN

St. Elizabeth Catholic Church is located in an urban, working-class neighborhood twenty minutes from downtown Detroit. According to parish priest Father Charles Morris, they are "not super rich," or in a rural area where being off the grid might seem more logical, and they are not in a year-round sunny climate. Even so, St. Elizabeth has managed to green their 9,000-square-foot rectory and their 16,200-square-foot church/school complex. It started with an energy audit in 1997, and by 2001 they had installed their first solar panels. Now a four-part energy system supplies between 30 percent and 40 percent of the rectory's energy needs. Computers, printers, lights, and televisions are powered by renewable energy. Power outages caused by winter storms sometimes go unnoticed for a while in the building that serves as a residence and also houses church offices. "During the blackout, we kept on trucking," said Father Morris. The water stays hot, lights work, and computers operate.

Solar attic fans help cool the rectory on sunny days, a solar/thermal collector provides the energy for hot water, and a hybrid system of photovoltaic panels and a wind turbine power many of the lights and electronic equipment. Father Morris is quick to emphasize that reducing their carbon footprint is not all about high tech actions. It begins with insulating well, caulking, changing lights to compact fluorescents, and turning down the heat. He suggests doing these easy things first — changes that cost little or no money, but provide an energy savings return. "If you can seal a crack, seal it."

Father Morris said that because of the changes made at St. Elizabeth, "we reduced our peak energy demand by 60 percent in five years. As a consequence, our utility dropped their demand charge by another $300/month. A nice perk for doing the right thing."

His suggestions for other churches looking to decrease their energy use, reduce carbon emissions, and save money at the same time are:

* start with an energy assessment or audit to "get the lay of the land"

* first make no-cost and low-cost changes to reduce energy consumption

* develop and work within a five- or ten-year plan

* track your savings and reinvest saved money in further energy-saving measures

The faith-based perspective of caring for creation motivated Fr. Morris to spearhead changes at St. Elizabeth, but he was also responding to the practical aspects of being a pastor: "I have to pay the bills, too." Energy reduction measures appeal to both the environmentalists in the congregation and to those more focused on fiscal matters. With implementation of initiatives such as theirs, both groups "can sing out of the same hymnbook." He knows that many churches, especially older inner city ones like St. Elizabeth, have financial challenges, but when you can save money and do the right thing, it's a win-win situation. "Do it because it is the righteous thing to do, and do it because it will also save you money."

> St. Elizabeth Catholic Church
> 123 Goodell St.
> Wyandotte, MI 48192
> (734) 284-7727; (888) 288-8207
> *www.ste-wyan.org*

FAITH IN (COLLABORATIVE) ACTION

When I spoke with Rev. Amy Bowden Freedman in the spring of 2008, her church was working on becoming certified by the Unitarian Universalist Church as a "Green Sanctuary." The action plan was almost ready for submission to the national office, and the congregation's commitment to environmental stewardship had been evident for years. "[As Unitarians] our connection to nature has always been there." In fact, their historic church, Channing Memorial Church in Newport, Rhode Island, was named in memory of William E. Channing, the founder of Unitarianism in America. The congregation was organized by Channing in 1835, and the present building dates back to 1880, when it was built as part of the centennial celebration of his birth. Channing was a staunch social reformer; he was an abolitionist and was a proponent of free speech, education, peace, and caring for the poor. Early Unitarian Ralph Waldo Emerson called him "a kind of public Conscience," and he was said to have inspired another Unitarian, naturalist, advocate for simple living, and inspiration to environmentalists for 150 years, Henry David Thoreau.

So the roots of caring for the Earth run deep with Unitarians and with Channing Memorial Church. Rev. Freedman said the "energetic people" of the church are "action oriented." Their actions have included joining with another local church, Portsmouth United Methodist, to hold a rally in April 2007 as part of the first nationwide "Step It Up National Day of Climate Action." The goal of Step It Up is to get the U.S. Congress to commit to cutting U.S. carbon emissions 80 percent by 2050. The rally at Easton's Beach, on Aquidneck Island where Newport is located, featured speakers including their U.S. Senator, a local fishermen, musicians, ministers, environmentalists, and an area businessman who is making biodiesel fuel from used grease from local restaurants. The rally was important for drawing attention to the issue of the climate crisis, for bringing the issue close to home by educating the public on how global warming is affecting the local shoreline and economy, and for offering solutions to the problems. But according to Rev. Freedman, the rally's other important message was that solutions take collaboration — between Channing Memorial and Portsmouth Methodist; between churches and the larger community; between politicians and business people, between Rhode Island and the other states, and actually with the rest of the world. For Rev. Freedman, "the sacred and the secular are very closely aligned"; for her congregation, social, economic, and environmental justice and political actions are all part of their spiritual lives. From one of her sermons:

> *In reverence for the beauty of the Earth and the sacredness of all living beings, human beings must resolve to work together to change the way we live... we want to find ways to join with people beyond our congregation to form partnerships and make a difference together.... It's easy being green because morally and spiritually there is no alternative.*

Channing Memorial Church
135 Pelham St.
Newport, RI 02840-3131
(401) 846-0643
www.channingchurch.org

ALOHA ʻĀINA

"It's all connected," said Wailani Robins, the director of programs and development at the Kawaiahaʻo Church School in Honolulu. As a native Hawaiian who has been on staff for eighteen years, she is acutely aware of the interconnectedness of Christianity, Hawaiian culture, and Earth care. "It all works together" — loving one another, taking care of each other, and taking care of the Earth. "What better way to take care of each other than to take care of the environment?" Love, respect, and care of others and of the natural world are taught through lessons, cultural practices, and example. "We instill a way of life here for the children."

The school is owned and operated by Kawaiahaʻo Church, the first Christian church on the island of Oʻahu. In the 1820s, missionaries were granted an area of arid land around a freshwater spring. Prior to the missionaries' arrival, the spring was reserved for use by high chiefs and chiefesses; the church name comes from a chiefess named Haʻo. *Ka Wai a Haʻo* in Hawaiian means the freshwater pool of Haʻo. The church was originally a thatched structure lined with mats. In 1838 the foundation was begun for the church that continues today to be of great spiritual, cultural, and historical value to the people of Hawaiʻi. The church was made of thousand-pound slabs of ocean coral that were chiseled by natives of the land from underwater reefs. About fourteen thousand of these slabs were brought to the water's surface and carried in canoes to the church site. King Kamehameha III and five thousand others were present at the dedication of the church in 1842. The rich history of this iconic church is woven into the fiber of the Kawaiahaʻo Church School.

Infants through fifth-graders reap the benefits of the integration of spirituality, Hawaiian culture, and environmentalism at the school. A typical school day begins with the children and staff gathering for song and *pule* (prayer), and with this "Pledge to the Earth":

I pledge allegiance to the Earth and to all life that it nourishes: all growing things, all species of animals, and all races of people. I promise to protect all life on our planet, to live in harmony with nature, and to share our resources justly so that all people can live with dignity, in good health, and in peace."

The pledge and the school logo adorn reusable shopping bags that the school sells as a fundraising project. Their first monetary donation from this endeavor was presented in May 2008 to the nonprofit organization Friendship Caravan for their Amman Imman ("Water Is Life") program to help fund the building of water wells for the Azawak people of Niger. Future funds raised by the sale of the shopping bags will go to the "Water for Life" program of the United Nations. The goals of this decade long project (2005–2015) are to increase access to safe drinking water and basic sanitation to people worldwide and to end the exploitation of water resources. Providing water to those who lack access — a fitting cause for a church and school so tied to water through their freshwater spring and the ocean's gift of coral.

While the kids of Kawaiahaʻo Church School are learning their connection to others and to the natural world around the globe, they are also learning their connection to nature close to home. Their learning spaces flow seamlessly from indoors to outdoors. Each classroom is named for a local plant, and they store their shoes in reused plastic flower pots in wooden shoe shelves painted with a picture of the classroom plant. They tend small gardens and learn the names, parts, and uses of the mostly native plants they grow. They eat bananas from their trees, use the dye from native plant berries in art projects, and grow *kalo* (taro), one of the most culturally important plants of ancient and present-day Hawaiians. They compost the remains of their lunches and recycle cans and bottles. This is part of a normal day for these children who are the future of the islands. As Wailani said, the kids and staff go about their days, "all the while talking about the beautiful things God gave us to take care of." Their vision statement: *Aloha Ke Akua, Aloha Kekahi i Kekahi, Aloha ʻĀina.* Love God, Love One Another, Love the Land.

Kawaiahaʻo Church School
872 Mission Lane
Honolulu, HI 96813
(808) 585-0622
www.kawaiahaoschool.com

A NATURAL SANCTUARY

A 2004 National Council of Churches training conference — "H2oly Water: Source of Life" — inspired members of several churches in Maryland to begin thinking more about their connection to the water of the Chesapeake Bay and to the water of the Earth in general. Urban sprawl, overdevelopment, industrial and agricultural chemicals, home lawn chemicals, vehicle residues, and inadequate municipal water treatment facilities all contribute to pollution of water resources. With awareness of this, members of churches in the Baltimore–Annapolis area joined together and formed Chesapeake Covenant Congregations with the goal of protecting the land and water of the Chesapeake Bay watershed ecosystem. Each congregation is encouraged to write its own covenant for caring for the Earth.

Members of the Maryland Presbyterian Church (MPC) in the northern suburbs of Baltimore had already been active in environmental stewardship, addressing how their actions as individuals and as a congregation affect the Earth. Their Environmental Stewardship Action Group provides leadership in this area of ministry. In what Bill Breakey, a member of the group, called a "wonderful process that involved the whole church," they drafted a covenant "with each other and with God and with Earth itself" to reduce energy use, find solutions to environmental injustices, use sustainable practices at home, work, and church, and partner with other groups to promote environmental stewardship. Their beautifully named "Covenant to Enjoy and Care for Earth Community" was posted on Earth Day Sunday 2008, and members of the congregation were given the opportunity during the worship service to sign it and so to pledge their individual and group Earth-care intentions.

Though their covenant formalized and articulated their beliefs and pledged practices, the congregation had been busily working on environmental stewardship projects for years. According to Bill, the Environmental Stewardship Action Group determined that "if we are trying to improve the Earth, maybe we should start by trying to improve our own little piece of earth." This close-to-home thinking has spawned several on-going projects, some of which are directly related to their enviable natural setting.

MPC sits on over four acres of wooded land in suburban Baltimore. Oak and tulip poplar trees grace this land. Unfortunately, as has happened in many other native ecosystems around the country, non-native, invasive plant species have infiltrated the area. Alien plants such as garlic mustard, wineberry, English ivy, pachysandra, and others had taken hold at the expense of native plants. The MPC environmental stewards built a nature trail to allow folks to walk through and enjoy the woods, and they have instituted an on-going program of weeding out non-native plants and of planting native species. While simultaneously working in concert with others at the regional level and while recognizing their responsibility for global environmental stewardship, they are "trying to restore our own little bit of nature."

This restoration is tough work and made even more challenging by the tremendous damage done by the beautiful but overabundant white-tailed deer that frequent the woodland. The hungry deer have posed a problem to the reestablishment of native plants, but the problem has been addressed by the ecologically harmonious measure of researching and finding natives that are "unattractive" to the deer — and thereby discouraging their destructive behavior naturally.

Though MPC is blessed with acres of beautiful (and now increasingly restored) land, some of the land is of course covered over with their building and parking lot. Building and paving over land alters the natural cycle of precipitation being filtered by the soil into the ground water, then entering the flowing water and ocean, evaporating, and falling again. In some urban areas, two-thirds of precipitation falls on built-over surfaces. The ensuing runoff pollutes and overflows streams, causes erosion, and overtaxes sewage systems. MPC wanted to mitigate the negative effects of their paved and built surfaces, and though replacing the impermeable paving was not ecologically reasonable or financially feasible, other measures were taken. To diminish the effects of heavy snow and rain water, including pollution of the local streams and rivers and ultimately the Chesapeake Bay, MPC installed a rain garden. This was no easy task and involved earth-moving equipment and engineering skills. To finance the project, they applied for and received a grant from the Chesapeake Bay Trust. In addition, a young member of the congregation who is an Eagle Scout also received a grant — this one to add natural coir fiber logs to an area experiencing heavy storm water runoff from the parking lot. One foot in diameter and ten to twenty feet long, these logs were placed along the contour of the garden slope to slow the force of storm water, which allows it then to be more easily absorbed by the soil. This results in better water filtration, less erosion, and less pollution entering the waterways. The coir logs also serve to capture sediment and provide a place for vegetation to become established.

Not every congregation has an annual "Garlic Mustard Pull," but MPC does. They persistently weed out these invasive plants along with other non-natives. One Sunday a month following worship, dedicated MPC-ers also have an "eco-party," during which they continue their planting and tending and their ecologically friendly (i.e., pesticide-free) efforts of eradicating non-native plants — by hand and one invasive plant at a time. Hard work? Yes. Tedious weeding? Probably. Worth it? Absolutely.

This natural area is a living testament to the MPC Covenant, which in part reads,

> *When caring for the grounds we will take care to restore, protect, and enhance their beauty and their natural resources, while creating a sanctuary for God's creatures who share our neighborhood and our Earth.*

Maryland Presbyterian Church
1105 Providence Rd.
Towson, MD 21286
(410) 825-0719
www.mpchurch.org

Chesapeake Covenant Congregations
www.chesapeakecovenant.org

ZERO TRASH LUNCHES

Unitarian Universalist congregations are known not only for their *commitment* to social justice, but also for their related *actions*. A Unitarian church was founded in 1821 in the very heart of Washington, D.C. This historic church (now known as All Souls Church) has a tradition of extraordinary social justice actions, and this legacy sets a high standard for the current congregation.

Early ministers of the church spoke out against slavery. During the Civil War, church members volunteered to help wounded soldiers when the building served as a hospital. And during World War I, the congregation supported the efforts of the Red Cross, including supplying them with an ambulance. Early in the 1900s, the church dining room was one of the only places in Washington where racially integrated groups were served. Because of this, Eleanor Roosevelt and others held meetings there, and these early desegregation efforts set the stage for later church work in the civil rights movement. From the 1930s through the 1950s, the church was the site of many youth clubs and school programs. In the 1950s, '60s, and '70s, civil rights activism played an important role in the life of the church. And in 1965 a former assistant All Souls Church (ASC) minister was murdered during the civil rights protests in Selma, Alabama. Several years later the first ASC African-American senior minister was hired. After the assassination of Dr. Martin Luther King Jr., the church formed a housing corporation to rebuild neighboring inner-city housing laid waste during the subsequent riots. In the 1970s, members of the congregation demonstrated against South Africa apartheid. And throughout the years the church has been active in peace-making activities. Saying that ASC has a rich history of social justice actions is a considerable understatement. That the people who inherited this strong and enduring tradition of social justice are also becoming known for their environmental justice commitment and actions is no surprise.

Unitarians have seven guiding principles, the last of which is "respect for the interdependent web of all existence of which we are a part." The ASC "7th Principle Committee" (or Green Souls) spearheads multiple environmental stewardship initiatives, and ASC wholeheartedly embraces the ethic of "Reduce-Reuse-Recycle." They have a RideShare program; hold an annual Green Transport Day to encourage members to walk, bike, car pool, or take public transportation to church; recycle beverage containers; reduce their energy consumption; sell Fair Trade Certified organic coffee, tea, chocolate, and olive oil; and also sell energy-efficient light bulbs, environmentally safe cleaning products, and toilet paper and notebook paper with recycled content.

According to Lina Parikh, co-chair of the Green Souls, ASC has a "really diverse congregation" — with people of different racial-ethnic identities, ages, sexual orientations, religious beliefs, and abilities — numbering about 800. And on most Sundays throughout the year, 100 to 150 people stay after worship for lunch, which is prepared in the church kitchen. Besides the good food (which always includes a vegetarian option) and the opportunity to socialize with interesting people, these gatherings are noteworthy because they are now "Zero Trash" (ZT) lunches.

Years ago, after conducting a "waste audit," they realized that a tremendous amount of waste was being generated each week at their lunches. And so according to Lina, in 2003 they began "trying to minimize the amount of waste at the church." They estimated that 750 plates, cups, forks, knives, and napkins were disposed of each week following the lunches. The goal of creating *no* trash was then (and continues to be) accomplished by using real dishes and flatware, and by using fabric napkins made by members of the congregation. Initially the lunches were ZT once per quarter; in 2004, they stepped up their waste reduction efforts, and lunches became ZT twice per month. Since the fall of 2006, ZT lunches have become a weekly event. Making them ZT, rather than using disposables and pitching everything into trash cans at the end of the meal, is a decidedly more time- and labor-intensive way of serving the food — but the Green Souls believe it is definitely the way to go.

Lina described a rotating system of volunteers who each help once a month with the work related just to the dishes. Approximately seven people are needed to take the dishes out of the cupboards, bus the tables, load the dishwasher, and restock the pantry shelves with the clean dishes. This is in addition to the folks who prep, cook, and serve the food.

Though getting a sufficient number of volunteers can sometimes be a challenge, ASC remains committed to ZT. Lina said the gradual phase-in approach was one of the keys to their success.

"We didn't do everything at once — so it wasn't overwhelming. It was doable." While creating a more beautiful table setting and more pleasant dining experience, ASC has reduced landfill-bound paper and plastic trash by about thirty thousand items per year. At the same time, they are demonstrating that the old ways are sometimes the best ways.

The people of ASC are quite busy, quite green, and striving to become even greener. They educate themselves about global warming, reduce their energy consumption, make individual "Green Resolutions," implement their congregation-wide Green Sanctuary Action Plan, promote economic justice by buying and selling fair trade products — and they do their part to reduce the overflowing municipal waste stream.

ASC Zero Trash lunches: conceived, approached, advanced, and accomplished.

All Souls Church
1500 Harvard St. NW
Washington, DC 20009
(202) 332-5266
www.all-souls.org

DEEP GREEN

After I heard the story of the green building renovation of the Friends Center in downtown Philadelphia, the word that kept coming to mind was "change": The change that occurred in the thinking and perspective of Center staff that enabled them to go so comprehensively green in such a huge project. The change they engender in the thinking and possibly in the actions of others. The change (i.e., reduction) in the Center's electric and water bills. The seasonal changes in colors of their vegetated roof. And the change from gray, the color long associated with the Quaker principle of simplicity, to a very deep Quaker green, the color now associated with the Friends Center.

The group of three buildings that comprise the Friends Center includes the large and historic meetinghouse built in 1856, a large office building, and space for conferences and activities of the many nonprofit community organizations that utilize the Center. No significant renovation had been done at the Center since the 1970s, and early into the new century, the need for major work was evident. Patricia McBee is a member of the Quaker meeting at the heart of Friends Center, and the person who has led the fundraising campaign for what was to evolve into a massive project. According to Patricia, when the idea of building with sustainability in mind was introduced, the initial reaction was not encouraging. "In general, people said it's going to be too expensive, too complicated, too hard." But after deliberation and discussion, they decided to go forward — at least to explore the possibility. They applied for and received a $75,000 Kresge Foundation grant just to study how the buildings could be greened. And so by 2004, the Friends were brainstorming the possibilities with each other and with professionals. The results of a cost-benefit analysis that evaluated standard renovation against green renovation over the long term convinced them that sustainability was cost effective. The initial financial outlay was greater (no insignificant matter in a project of this magnitude), but the twenty-year bottom line was that going the green building route would save them $5 million. As others around the globe are increasingly realizing, planet-friendly is also pocketbook-friendly. Equally important to them is the huge reduction in their environmental footprint on the Earth. So they set out to create buildings that are completely fossil-fuel-free and carbon neutral, protect the watershed, are healthy places to work and worship, and are a witness to conscience and commitment. No small task. Especially when you consider they were planning to retrofit old buildings located in the middle of a city.

Patricia McBee told me that "nearly every issue of peace and social justice ties back to environmental degradation." The Quaker testimonies of peace, equality, simplicity, and integrity guide the daily actions of Friends and are all linked to their choices related to the renovation. Extricating themselves from the fossil fuel trap removes their need for those natural resources that are currently, and predicted to be in the future, the underlying cause of wars — and so they support *peace*. *Equality* translates into not continuing to gobble up more than their fair share of the planet's resources at the expense of the Earth and disproportionately at the expense of people in its poorer regions. *Simplicity* is a Quaker hallmark and is expressed in the green renovation by the focus on living in harmony with the Earth's natural systems of light, heat, and precipitation. And *integrity* requires putting into action their commitments to peace, equality, and simplicity by aligning their commitments and actions.

The Friends Center's green actions are numerous and splendid. The decision to preserve the old buildings instead of constructing new was an important first step. Recycling of the construction waste has kept it out of the landfill. Installing insulation reduces energy needs in a climate that sees extremes of both heat and cold. An open floor plan design and new windows make good use of natural light. The Center implements individual and office practices to reduce energy consumption, and the Center is able to purchase wind power for some of the energy they use. Photovoltaic panels provide some electricity, and because the solar array generates electricity during hot summer days, a time when there is high demand for electricity to cool buildings, the Center is helping to reduce the peak loads that are responsible for brown-outs and the demand for more power plants. And there is more....

A rather dramatic action they have taken is the drilling of very deep wells at the Center for geothermal heat exchange. Wells six inches in diameter and one thousand to fifteen hundred feet deep provide access to ground water that is consistently about fifty degrees. The deep well system exchanges the temperature of the water with the air temperature of the building. In the summer, the building is cooled as excess building heat is absorbed by the earth; conversely, in the winter, the system compresses the heat of the earth and transfers it to warm the building. Who knew? The system is "400 percent efficient," meaning that for every unit of electricity needed to operate it, four units of heat or cooling are produced.

Another notable green action at the Center is, well, actually green — and yellow and red and purple. In June of 2007, the roof of the office building became a garden roof. First the old black tar roof was replaced with an Energy Star–qualified white roof. Then solar panels were installed. Drainage medium and planting medium were added next, and finally tiny sedums were planted. Only one inch in diameter at planting, these low-maintenance and drought-resistant cuties grew to twelve inches in less than six months. The ten-thousand-square-foot "vegetated roof" serves to cool the building and to cool the air around the building, and so reduces the Center's contribution to the "urban heat island" (that is, higher city temperatures related to urban development). The green roof can be up to fifty degrees cooler than a black tar roof. In addition to the environmental benefits of the cooling effect in warm weather, it is financially beneficial because it insulates the building in both cold and hot weather. And the vegetated roof is expected to last two to three times as long as a nonvegetated roof; the plants stand up to the elements and protect the roofing from being exposed to and deteriorated by the sun's UV rays. The green roof protects the waterways from excess and polluted storm water runoff by absorbing at least 90 percent of the precipitation that falls on it, and it filters any water not absorbed.

Besides the fossil-fuel savings, the heat island reduction, and the financial benefits, the roof is "just so gorgeous," according to Patricia. Though it was designed to be low maintenance and a model of Quaker-appropriate simplicity, the roof is nevertheless a stunning standout in their city center neighborhood. The vegetated roof is on a three-story building surrounded by many highrises. The office workers, apartment dwellers, and hotel guests look down on what has been called (rather oxymoronically) a "Quaker neon sign." The sedums are green and yellow in the spring and summer, and they bloom purple and yellow and red. In the fall, they turn deep maroon and orange — a lovely display for those lucky enough to see it. The roof is "silent speech to anyone who looks out their window."

The message of that silent speech is the same message that Patricia gives verbally when she takes people on a tour of the Friends Center or gives one of her many presentations. "Who knew that our buildings are putting out twice as much CO_2 as our cars?" Well, she knows better than most of us now, and she is spreading the word. She has talked with hundreds of architects, building professionals, policy makers, landscape design students, and others about global warming, green building, and sustainability. And she has the knowledge, experience, and tangible evidence to share. "We would like to use our projects to help other people come to look at their buildings differently." Patricia said that now that those at the Center understand the detrimental impact of buildings on the planet, "We don't have any choice but to pay attention to how we're living on this Earth, and to take action."

Storm water runoff is a huge problem in the area. Philadelphia's combined sewer system becomes overburdened by storm water, causing raw sewage to be released into the Delaware River watershed more than fifty times a year. The roof of the meetinghouse will not become a vegetated roof due to the building's historic status, but even so, this roof, which is red in color, is decidedly green in use. The precipitation that falls on it is captured, collected in tanks, and pumped over to the office building where it is used to flush the toilets — thereby reducing the Center's city water use (and their water bill) by 90 percent, once again demonstrating that being Earth-friendly equates with fiscal responsibility.

The Friends Center changes are quite impressive — but trying to impress others is not what Quakers do. Nonetheless they do model behavior that supports peace, justice, equality, and simplicity, and that inspires others. As they go fossil-fuel free at the Friends Center, they are purposefully fueling green change in Philadelphia, and much farther afield. Their showcase of sustainability speaks loud and clear to those of us who listen.

Friends Center Corporation
1501 Cherry St.
Philadelphia, PA 19102
(215) 241-7190
www.friendscentercorp.org

Appendix

Theology, Psychology, and Ecology

THEOLOGY

"In the beginning God created the heaven and the earth" (Gen. 1:1). This alone seems reason enough for Christians to care for the Earth. If it seems insufficient, however, the Bible provides plenty more. Genesis speaks of the land, seas, grass, herbs, trees, seeds, whales, and every living creature, fowl, air, cattle, and even every creeping thing. And "it was very good" (Gen. 1:31). According to Genesis, humans were given "dominion" over "every living thing," and this passage is sometimes cited as reason for humans to be able to own or rule over the Earth. Theologians and others have studied these references to "dominion" in depth, and varying interpretations have emerged. J. M. Sleeth (2006) writes that the original Hebrew word means "higher on the root of a plant" and more likely implies human dependency on everything that is under us. If the root of a plant is destroyed, the plant does not blossom or give fruit. If the Earth is destroyed, humans are also doomed. T. Hiebert (2000) reviews scholarly thought on this and related verses and presents another interpretation. God created man (Gen. 2:7), *adam*, from *adama* (or *adamah*), ground, or more precisely, arable land or topsoil. Plants (Gen. 2:9) and animals (Gen. 2:19) are also made out of the same *adama* — and so humans are "not distinguished from other forms of life but identified with them." And the work of humans is to till, cultivate, or "keep" the garden (Gen. 2:15).

Humans have a biblical mandate to care for all that God created, not to lord over it, use it up, degrade, or disrespect it. In fact, the first verse of Psalm 24 says, "The earth is the Lord's and the fullness thereof; the world, and they that dwell therein." Psalm 96:11–12 reads, "Let the heavens rejoice and let the earth be glad; let the sea roar, and the fullness thereof. Let the field be joyful, and all that is therein; then shall all the trees of the wood rejoice." According to the Bible, God put Adam in the Garden of Eden to tend it, and God commanded Noah to save animal and human life on the planet by building an ark. Toward the end of the Bible we read, "thou...shouldest destroy them which destroy the earth" (Rev. 11:18). Many more examples exist, and biblical scholars and writers make a strong case for the biblical mandate of caring for God's creation. C. B. DeWitt (1994) in his book *Earth-Wise: A Biblical Response to Environmental Issues* says that human actions that contribute to ozone destruction and global warming, deforestation, species extinction, and other environmental problems are "creation degradations" and "are contrary to biblical teachings." He goes on to say,

> The Bible is hardly a minor contributor when it comes to providing advice on caring for creation. In fact, the Bible provides such powerful environmental teachings that it can be thought of as a kind of ecological handbook on how to rightly live on earth.... The Bible's serious treatment of environmental matters should not surprise us. Since God created and sustains all of creation we should expect the Bible to call us to bring honor to God. We should expect the Scriptures to support creation's proper care and keeping and to encourage us to maintain the integrity of the creation. (39–40)

In *Saving God's Green Earth* (2006), pastor Tri Robinson writes,

> God speaks to all of us in many different ways, yet it's through nature that He so easily grabs our attention. Among other things, Jesus primarily saw nature as a way of illuminating the Gospel and elements that are central to our faith. Parables of seeds, crops, soil, and trees abound in Jesus' teaching, unfolding deep spiritual truths and revealing elements about God's nature. ... If there's so much beauty in nature and we experience God speaking to us through it, doesn't it make sense that the church should lead the way in caring for the environment? (43–44)

In *Serve God, Save the Planet: A Christian Call to Action* (2006), Sleeth advises the reader to "keep in our hearts this thought: God created the earth, and if we do not respect the earth and all of its creatures, we disrespect God." He reminds us that caring for the least among us is a biblical mandate, and writes that "environmental concerns are intimately tied to issues of poverty, health, and compassion" (26). "Unspoken reasons for neglecting our role as stewards include greed, thoughtlessness, lust, exploitation, and short-term profit. These factors negatively affect our environment as well as our individual walk with God" (34).

The National Council of Churches of Christ (NCC) Eco-Justice program is clear in its statements about Christian environmental stewardship. One illustration of this comes from their publication "Bottom Line Ministries That Matter: Congregational Stewardship with Energy Efficiency and Clean Energy Technologies":

> As people of God, Christians are called to care for God's gracious gift of creation. Christians are called to be moral images of God and to reflect God's divine love and justice through "keeping" the Garden (Gen. 2:15). This special relationship with God requires good stewardship of God's creation. Christian concern should extend beyond humanity

to encompass the whole of creation — from rivers and oceans to fields and mountains....

The world is increasingly bound together as a global community. Christians are called to create right relationships, both social and ecological, with all of God's creation. The burning of fossil fuels for energy use disproportionately impacts the health of communities of color, people living in poverty, and children. People of faith have the opportunity to put their faith in action to create a more just, sustainable world through their energy choices. (Anderson-Stembridge and Radford (n.d.)

The NCC website also provides an "Anthology of Environmental Statements" from denominations including the American Baptist Church, Christian Church (Disciples of Christ), Church of the Brethren, Episcopal Church, Evangelical Lutheran Church in America, Friends United Meeting, Orthodox Church, Moravian Church in America, National Council of Churches, Philadelphia Yearly Meeting, Presbyterian Church USA, Reformed Church in America, United Church of Christ, and the United Methodist Church.

The policies, resolutions, and statements documented in this anthology are striking in their early, forward-thinking, and forthright calls for people of faith unequivocally to be stewards of the natural environment. A few examples among many:

• The Episcopal Church's 66th General Convention in 1979 "calls every Member of this Church to exercise a responsible life style based on real personal needs commensurate with a world of limited resources by:

  1. Conserving energy in our homes, jobs, parishes, communities, travels, and leisure activities.

  2. Altering our own eating and consumption habits.

  3. Planning family size in a responsible manner."

The 70th General Convention of the Episcopal Church in 1991 resolved "to protect the sanctity of the Arctic National Wildlife Refuge in Alaska by opposing the opening of this refuge for oil development," "support the reauthorization of the Endangered Species Act by the Congress," and affirmed "our responsibility for the earth in trust for this and future generations" declaring "that Christian Stewardship of God's created environment, in harmony with our respect for human dignity, requires response from the Church of the highest urgency."

◆ A Presbyterian Church USA denominational statement on Natural Resources as early as 1954 called upon "the Christian conscience to recognize that our stewardship of the earth and water involves both a land-use program which recognizes the interdependence of soil, water and man and the development of a responsible public policy which will resist the exploitation of land, water, and other natural resources, including forests, for selfish purposes and maintain intelligent conservation for the sustenance of all living creatures through future generations."

The PC (USA) General Assembly in 2003 called on "the United States government to join in the world effort to reduce greenhouse gas emissions, and to develop and enact a national emergency response, underwritten by law, with adequate financial support, and economic enforcement mechanisms, to be fully functioning by 2005, with targeted reductions by that time" ... and to "direct the Stated Clerk to communicate this concern to the president of the United States, and all appropriate government authorities."

And in an amazingly forward-thinking and forward-*moving* action, the PC (USA) General Assembly in 2006 called for its members to become "carbon neutral." The Presbyterian Hunger Program links carbon emissions to global warming, and global warming to increased hunger among the poor. Their tips on becoming carbon neutral include calculating one's own carbon emissions, decreasing energy usage by traveling less, eating less meat, buying energy-efficient cars and electronics, and purchasing carbon offsets (Presbyterian Hunger Program 2007).

• The Reformed Church in America in 1977 adopted a resolution urging "the constituency of the Reformed Church in America to exercise responsible stewardship with regard to the use of energy in the light of the crisis that exists, by putting conservation methods into practice in whatever ways possible."

In its 1993 "Call to Action," the Reformed Church wrote, "We call upon the church to promote integrity for the creation, to restore broken relationships, and to equip men and women of God to act wisely, creatively, and redemptively. What can we do? What must we do, in the name of the one who created and who redeems, for the sake of future generations and for the sake of the creation itself? The greatest priority must be to reduce the use of fossil fuels, particularly coal and oil. At an individual level we must reduce our automobile use, purchase products and appliances which take less energy to produce and which consume less energy in operation, and participate with others in community activities designed to conserve resources and to protect the environment. Churches, too, can play a positive role with wise purchases and an active educational effort to inform members about the causes and consequences of global warming and the steps that are necessary to reduce this danger."

• The United Methodist Church in 1984 in "Theology of Stewardship and the Environment" stated, "All creation is under the authority of God and all creation is interdependent. Our covenant with God requires us to be stewards, protectors, and defenders of all creation." It goes on to say, "In the Bible, a steward is one given responsibility for what belongs to another. The Greek word we translate as steward is *oikonomos,* one who cares for the household or acts as its trustee. The word *oikos,* meaning household, is used to describe the world as God's household. Christians, then, are to be stewards of the whole household (creation) of God. *Oikonomia,* 'stewardship,' is also the root of our word 'economics.' Oikos, moreover, is the root of our modern word, 'ecology.' Thus in a broad sense, stewardship, economics, and ecology are, and should be, related. The Old Testament relates these concepts in the vision of shalom. Often translated 'peace,' the broader meaning of shalom is wholeness. In the Old Testament, shalom is used to characterize the wholeness of a faithful life lived in relationship to God. Shalom is best understood when we experience wholeness and harmony as human beings with God, with others, and with creation itself."

In "Our Social Principles," the United Methodist Church states, "All creation is the Lord's and we are responsible for the ways in which we use and abuse it. Water, air, soil, minerals, energy resources, plants, animal life, and space are to be valued and conserved because they are God's creation and not solely because they are useful to human beings. God has granted us stewardship of creation. We should meet these stewardship duties through acts of loving care and respect" (National Council of Churches of Christ Eco-Justice Programs 2007).

Many other denominations have weighed in on the matter. Bartholomew I, archbishop of Constantinople, ecumenical patriarch, and spiritual leader of 250 million Orthodox Christians worldwide, has led numerous conferences on environmental stewardship. He said in April 2005 that the first five meetings in their series of summer ecological seminars (1994–99) "established that the protection of the environment in which humanity lives is a divine commandment.... For the pollution or destruction of a single element of the environment brings hardship on the life of another.... Consequently, there is an ethical responsibility on our part that we not make life difficult for our fellow human beings." He went on to say that "tending and protecting the earthly environment...is a commandment of God...a religious obligation" (Ecumenical Patriarchate 2005).

In 2006 Pope Benedict XVI said members of the Catholic Church "in dialogue with Christians of various churches...need to commit ourselves to caring for the created world, without squandering its resources, and [share] them in a cooperative way" (Catholic News Service 2006). The pope led a 2007 end-of-summer eco-friendly youth rally in Italy that drew hundreds of thousands of young people; the prayer books were made of recycled paper, hydrogen cars were on display, biodegradable plates were used, backpacks made from recycled nylon and containing hand-cranked battery chargers were given away, and trees were planted (to offset the rally's carbon emissions) in the area of the country that had recently been severely damaged by fires (MSNBC 2007).

And in September 2007, nearly two hundred environmental scientists, government officials, and religious leaders from all over the world met in Greenland at the mouth of a melting glacier to join in a silent prayer and to appeal to humankind to address the effects we humans are having on the planet. The meeting was sponsored by Ecumenical Patriarch Bartholomew , who said "there is no time for waiting or delay" and called for "repentance, together with the change of life that accompanies repentance" for the human actions that have led to environmental degradation. Pope Benedict sent his support and said environmental stewardship actions show "better respect for the wonders of God's creation" (Catholic News Service 2007). The pope's representative at the meeting, Cardinal Thomas McCarrick, was quoted as saying, "Whatever denomination we are we will try to proclaim loud and clear that we should, we must, pay attention to the water resources and climate change...I don't think we have any differences on this. Every religion realizes that this world is a gift from God" (ABC News 2007).

PSYCHOLOGY

The field of psychology studies humans and behavior and recognizes the importance of the interconnectedness of humans in creating a healthy life. Ecopsychology focuses on the relationship between environmental and personal well-being and recognizes that the psychological and physical health of humans is directly related to, and in fact impossible without, a healthy planet. Environmental psychologists focus on many and varied areas related to natural environments, built environments, and conservation behaviors, and they understand that environmental degradation is the result of human behavior (Clay 2001b). The psychological aspects of the task at hand (i.e., protecting and restoring the environment) are important in that understanding what people know, think, fear, and want provides information about how best to address issues. Understanding what persuades and motivates people to alter their behaviors makes positive action steps more likely to occur (Brown 1995). Psychology offers not only the "hows" of effecting environmental stewardship, but some additional "whys" of doing so.

The blending of psychology and ecology is synergistic in that the work of each discipline is enhanced by the knowledge of the other. Psychological well-being is tied to *intra*personal functioning (e.g., one's beliefs, values, feelings), *inter*personal functioning (e.g., connectedness to others, behaviors), and person-to-nature connections. Ecological well-being — the health of the planet — is directly tied to the actions of humans. Psychological principles, research, and knowledge inform the environmental movement, and some of the most valuable information from the field of psychology is that "shocking and shaming the public" is not the most effective tactic (Roszak, 1995, 15). Theodore Roszak, who is credited with coining the term "ecopsychology" in his book *The Voice of the Earth* (1992/2001), wrote in *Ecopsychology: Restoring the Earth, Healing the Mind:*

> The question of motivation sets the tone and shapes the tactics of every political program. Start from the assumption that people are greedy brutes, and the tone of all you say will be one of contempt. Assume that people are self-destructively stupid, and your tactics are apt to become overbearing at best, dictatorial at worst. As for those on the receiving end of the assumption, shame has always been among the most unpredictable motivations in politics; it too easily slides into resentment. Call someone's entire way of life into question, and what you are apt to produce is defensive rigidity. It is elementary psychology that those who wish to change the world for the better should not begin by vilifying the public they seek to persuade, or by confronting it with a task that appears impossible. (Roszak, 1995, 15–16)

"Sustainability" has become a frequently used term. In general it refers to the ability of an ecosystem to function well and to meet present needs without impairing its ability to meet the needs of future generations. Environmental programs that rely solely on creating public awareness of sustainability issues to bring about change are limited in their effect. Discovering the reasons why people do not engage in Earth-friendly actions is possible, as is knowing what "tools" to use to foster desired behavior changes. Using the right tools can greatly improve the effectiveness of environmental programs (McKenzie-Mohr and Smith 1999). In their book, *Fostering Sustainable Behavior,* the authors explain the reasons people do *not* adopt Earth-friendly activities, and then they present research-based strategies for increasing the chances that they will. Considering these strategies when planning and implementing church-based environmental programs is likely to result in more effective programs. According to McKenzie-Mohr and Smith (1999), the reasons people do *not* adopt environmentally friendly actions are because they:

1. are unaware of the environmental stewardship activity or of its benefits

2. are aware of it but perceive significant barriers to participating in the activity (e.g., it is too expensive, too unappealing, too inconvenient)

3. believe they benefit more by continuing their present behavior (e.g., it is easier)

However, people will generally engage in activities that they perceive have high benefits and few barriers, though benefits and barriers are different for different people. Groups, such as committees focusing on effecting positive environment-related changes in congregations, must consider which behaviors they want to address, and what situations people will confront when deciding whether to adopt a new behavior. Knowledge and attitudes have some bearing on action, but inconvenience will trump them both.

A "community-based social marketing" approach includes identifying the barriers (such as inconvenience) and benefits, designing and piloting a strategy, and then evaluating the results. Personal contact with those you want to adopt environmentally friendly activities is encouraged because research indicates that direct appeals and support of others is effective. Gleaning information about potential barriers and possible strategies from past studies, written reports, accounts of other groups' successful and unsuccessful attempts with similar populations, and through personal interviews, surveys, or focus groups is recommended.

Psychological research has also indicated effective "tools" to facilitate behavior change:

* *Commitment:* Seek commitments only for behaviors about which people have indicated an interest. These commitments can be verbal, but are more effective if written, given in public, or as a group. Encouraging people to complete pledge cards (as described in "Make an Offering to the Earth," page 95 above) is an example of using commitments to increase the likelihood of behavior change.

* *Prompts:* Make prompts easy to understand, such as signs to remind people to engage in a behavior. An example of a visual prompt is an easily seen and self-explanatory sign posted near the place the desired behavior should occur — such as a "Recycle your aluminum cans here" sign on a conveniently located receptacle, or a "Please turn out the lights when you leave" sign on the wall by the light switch.

* *Norms:* Focus on making the behavior the usual and accepted action by modeling the behavior and making it something that "we" (the members of the congregation) do. For example, to reduce the use of plastic-bottled water, start by educating the congregation about the perils of plastic bottles (through your newsletter); make it church policy no longer to purchase plastic-bottled water for church functions, and instead provide pitchers of water; and model the behavior of bringing your own reusable cups or travel mugs.

* *Communication:* Use ways of communicating information that capture attention, and people and methods that are credible. Focus on positive actions and results, provide or jointly develop goals, use personal contact to spread the word and discuss related issues, and provide feedback (e.g., how many trees were planted or how much energy and money was saved by energy conservation measures being enacted).

- *Incentives:* Consider "rewards" for behavior change (e.g., recognition in the newsletter, or rewards for the larger church community such as purchasing a tree to plant on church grounds with money generated from recycling). Intrinsic rewards, good feelings generated from within the individual, are more desirable, and are relatively easy to foster in members of faith communities who are accustomed to "doing good" just because it is the right thing to do.

- *Removal of external barriers:* Make environmentally friendly activities as easy and convenient as possible. When a sustainable behavior is perceived as or actually is too inconvenient or too expensive, this creates a barrier to implementation. To encourage recycling and reusing of church bulletins and inserts, for example, have easily accessible paper recycling containers located near the exits. Clearly indicate which containers are for which papers, and clearly mark any reusable materials so they can be placed in a "Reuse" container. Or if installing rather costly dimmable energy efficient light bulbs to replace the sanctuary's current dimmable bulbs is considered low priority and too expensive for the church to fund, implement an "adopt a light bulb" campaign so that those interested and able can fund individual light bulbs at the actual cost per bulbs. Print or post the names of those who fund the project. This also serves as a norm of supporting the use of the energy efficient bulbs and of funding their purchase. Note: Sometimes a project actually is too expensive or difficult to implement at the moment. In such cases, move on to a project that is manageable.

- *Design and evaluation:* Measure changes in behavior (e.g., increased paper recycling and decreased paper use resulting in a reduction in paper purchased) and cost savings (e.g., the decrease in the water bill after the installation of low-flush toilets), not changes in attitudes (which often don't reflect behavior changes). Modify programs that are not effective (McKenzie-Mohr and Smith 1999).

An additional note about two of these tools — norms and communication: Research shows that when the purpose of communication is to foster behavior change from environmentally harmful behavior to pro-environment behavior, the message should not emphasize "regrettably frequent" (i.e., common but undesirable) normative behavior (e.g., many people throw aluminum cans in the trash instead of recycling). Your message should instead emphasize that pro-environment behaviors are not only *desirable,* but that *people are engaging in them* (e.g., recycling cans saves resources and we are one of the many organizations that have active recycling programs). Therefore if you are trying to influence a specific behavior, be sure that your message does not inadvertently activate or reinforce a regrettably frequent norm, but that it is geared toward activating and reinforcing the norm of engaging in an accepted, desirable, and prevalent behavior (Cialdini 2003).

In addition to helping us understand *how* to move people toward environmentally friendly behaviors, psychology helps us understand *why* this is important. Natural environments can be restorative and help prevent and mitigate psychological stress (Kaplan 1995); promote post-surgery recovery; increase the ability of children to pay attention, delay gratification, and inhibit impulses; positively affect cognitive functioning; increase positive emotions and decrease anger and depression (Clay 2001a). Time in nature, including a retreat at a "spiritually rich, serene, and beautiful setting" of a monastery, has been shown to result in a meaningful restorative experience (Ouellette, Kaplan, and Kaplan 2005).

Other psychological research suggest that individuals who are "I"-centered or self-centered, as opposed to being community-centered, and those with personality traits of exploitativeness of entitlement (specific components of the psychological concept of narcissism) are likely to be disconnected from the natural world (Frantz, Mayer, Norton, and Rock 2005). Therefore, a decrease in self-absorption and an expansion of an individual's sense of self to include the natural world is important in addressing environmental problems. Expanding the concept of "self" through the development of a sense of identification with and interconnectedness to all beings and with the entire planet naturally leads to Earth/people-friendly behaviors (Conn 1995). Psychologists and others (educators, writers, religious leaders, artists, and people from many other walks of life) are engaged in the process of facilitating the human-to-nature connection.

The human–nature *dis*connect began after the Industrial Revolution, which led to society's ever-increasing dependence on fossil fuels. Blaming technology for our subsequent disconnection from nature might seem logical, but this is not accurate (Axelrod and Suedfeld 1995). Technology enables the rapid destruction of tropical rainforests to grow sun-cultivated coffee or to make furniture; we might never associate our relatively inexpensive coffee or coffee table with deforestation and its effect on global warming. Technology allows the development of innovative and useful items such as cell phones, computers, and MP3 players; as we buy, use, dispose of, and then buy the latest models, we might be totally disconnected from the knowledge that the production, transport, and disposal of these devices creates pollution in the air, water, and ground. Technology allows us to use refrigerators, air conditioners, and lights by flicking a switch, but that switch disconnects us from the source of the electricity — generally the fossil fuels of coal, oil and natural gas — and therefore from the knowledge that burning a light bulb means burning fossil fuels, which results in global warming. So technology is obviously a factor. But technology alone is not responsible for environmental problems. The *behavior of humans* and the choices societies make regarding technology's use are what determine the effects (Axelrod and Suedfeld

1995). In fact, technology, in its best forms such as in the creation of plant-based and biodegradable "plastics"; solar, wind, and wave power; sustainable farming techniques; biofuels; and low or no emission and fuel efficient vehicles, undoubtedly offers us the best alternatives to our current Earth-destructive practices.

Psychological concepts such as denial, alienation, narcissism, rationalization, and addiction that were developed to explain intrapersonal and interpersonal problems and behavior have more recently been applied to human–environment problems — denial of the destructive impact of our day-to-day actions; alienation from nature, so that we perceive ourselves as *apart from* nature instead of as *a part of* nature; narcissistic entitlement and rationalization of behaviors, and addiction to our energy and resource depleting lifestyles without thought to the consequences. Just as psychological methods of addressing personal and human-to-human relational problems can be effective, so this knowledge can help us develop and use a "relational psychology" to address human-to-planet relationship problems. This would be "experiencing in the deepest parts of our being, our connection with the Earth as sacred" (Mack 1995).

When we recognize the wonders of all of God's creation and know that we are *of* nature, then gratitude envelopes us and we reestablish the severed connection. As scientist David Suzuki (2007) writes, "Air is a place without borders or owners, shared by all life on Earth"; water is "a sacred liquid that links us to all the oceans of the world" and "flow[s] through our veins"; and earth is "the meadow we graze in, the ground we are shaped from, the daily bread that keeps body and soul together." "We *are* the air, we *are* the water, we *are* the earth."

ECOLOGY

Global warming has of late received significant attention in the popular press. My hope is that *of late* is not actually *too late*.

Though scientific evidence about global warming has been mounting for years, only relatively recently have the associated problems been given much consideration. In the United States this seems to be due to a lack of adequate governmental attention, and therefore a dearth of policies, laws, and programs to address the problem. The failure of our government to direct adequate attention to environmental issues during the past decade is well documented and unfortunate. The United States, with only 5 percent of the world's population, generates approximately 20 percent of the world's carbon dioxide emissions. Despite this we have not as of this writing signed the Kyoto Protocol, which is an extension of the United Nations Framework Convention on Climate Change (UNFCCC) international treaty. The Protocol "requires developed countries to reduce their GHG emissions below levels specified for each of them in the Treaty." These mandatory targets "must be met within a five-year time frame between 2008 and 2012, and add up to a total cut in GHG emissions of at least 5 percent against the baseline of 1990" (UNFCCC 2007a). Seeing the website's list (UNFCCC 2007b) of the 170-plus countries from Albania to Zambia (and most in between, including Canada, China, the European Union countries, Greece, Indonesia, India, and Japan) that have signed the Kyoto Protocol — and not seeing the United States among them is distressing. In addition to not joining the world in this effort, the United States in recent years has weakened environmental laws related to clean air and clean water. Nevertheless, blaming is not productive. Action is. And with enough call from the public, including the mounting groundswell from people of faith, green change in governmental policies and actions will increase.

Other factors contributing to the (so far) inadequate actions addressing global warming and related problems in our country include: social and economic systems based on consumerism; electronic and print media that until relatively recently largely ignored the issues; a shift over the past few decades toward single-use, short-lived, disposable, and plastic products; an increase in product packaging; a public uneducated about the issues and preoccupied with other things; and a growing alienation and disconnect from nature.

Consumerism, and the societal goals, beliefs, and values that support *over*consumption and *conspicuous* consumption of products, result in a "materialistic value orientation." This develops as a result of personal insecurities and doubts about one's self-worth, and as a result of exposure to materialistic values being modeled, valued, and promoted through advertising and by the behaviors of personal role models (e.g., family, friends) as well as public role models (e.g., sports figures, entertainers) (Kasser, Ryan, Couchman, and Sheldon 2004). Believing that self-worth is dependent on the acquisition and display of material possessions leads to overconsumption as a way of life. Interestingly enough, multiple studies have shown that people who have strong materialistic values report lower psychological well-being than those who do not hold these values (Kasser 2002).

Excessive consumerism has far-reaching environmental effects. Buying *more* products, be they electronic devices, jewelry, or furniture, and buying *bigger* versions of products, like SUVs and houses, magnifies the damaging effects on the environment. Every aspect of consumerism is implicated in the degradation of the planet's ecosystem. Natural resources (fossil fuels, forests, and water) are used in the production, packaging, transport, use, and disposal of products — and air, water, and ground pollution as well as climate change are the result. A simple equation:

$$\uparrow \text{consumption} = \uparrow \text{resource depletion} + \uparrow \text{pollution} = \uparrow \text{environmental damage}$$

Media attention, which has been sorely lacking, has significantly increased due to the attention generated by the release of *An Inconvenient Truth* in 2005. This movie shows Al Gore presenting his slide show of photos, diagrams, and scientific evidence on global warming. The movie, and the book of the same name (Gore 2006), resonated with the public, and much more coverage of environmental issues occurred in its wake. Articles addressing environmental issues began appearing regularly in newspapers, magazines, and denominational publications, and entire "green" issues of magazines proliferated. This has seemed to capture the attention of some new audiences and has led to increased awareness and education — and no doubt to at least some behavior change. Yet we need much more.

Why is more change necessary? The answer has come to light as media attention has focused on the work of the Intergovernmental Panel on Climate Change (IPCC). This body was established by the United Nations Environmental Programme and the World Meteorological Organization in 1988 to "assess on a comprehensive, objective, open, and transparent basis the latest scientific, technical, and socio-economic literature produced worldwide relevant to the understanding of the risk of human-induced climate change, its observed and projected impacts, and options for adaptation and mitigation" (IPCC 2007a). They draw on the work of hundreds of experts from around the world, assess in a "comprehensive, objective, open, and transparent basis," and produce reports consolidating their findings. IPCC reports released in 2007 made headlines. Some excerpts:

Warming of the climate system is unequivocal, as is now evident from observations of increases in global average air and ocean temperatures, widespread melting of snow and ice, and rising global average sea level.

At continental, regional, and ocean basin scales, numerous long-term changes in climate have been observed. These include changes in arctic temperatures and ice, widespread changes in precipitation amounts, ocean salinity, wind patterns and aspects of extreme weather including droughts, heavy precipitation, heat waves, and the intensity of tropical cyclones.

Palaeoclimatic information supports the interpretation that the warmth of the last half century is unusual in at least the previous 1,300 years. The last time the polar regions were significantly warmer than present for an extended period (about 125,000 years ago), reductions in polar ice volume led to 4 to 6 m of sea level rise.

Continued greenhouse gas emissions at or above current rates would cause further warming and induce many changes in the global climate system during the 21st century. (IPCC 2007d)

Based on years of accumulated scientific data the IPCC concluded that "global atmospheric concentrations of carbon dioxide, methane, and nitrous oxide have increased markedly *as a result of human activities*" (emphasis added). Even a quick perusal of the reports is enough to frighten any thinking person. Only lack of awareness, a highly activated denial defense, greed, or apathy could prevent one from being alarmed.

The IPCC reports make for some interesting reading as the scientists project global warming effects by geographical region and address issues related to precipitation, fresh water availability, resources, ecosystems, food/fiber/forest products, coral reefs, and other topics. These scientists project warmer average global temperatures, increases in heat waves, both heavy precipitation as well as more areas affected by droughts, increases in hurricanes and in sea levels. These climate changes are expected to result in crop decline; increased hunger and malnutrition; rises in surface ocean temperatures; death of corals; flooding of coastlines and coastal erosion; more deaths due to heat waves, floods, storms, fires, and droughts; increased cardio-respiratory diseases due to higher concentrations of ground level ozone; increased ground instability in permafrost regions and rock avalanches in mountain regions; changes in Arctic and Antarctic ecosystems; warming of lakes and rivers; and decreases in local food supplies (IPCC 2007b).

The evidence is in, the work has begun, and people of faith are well positioned to transform their lives and their congregations by being stewards of God's incredible creation.

Recommended Readings

Many books have been written in the often interrelated areas of theology, ecology, and psychology. The following recommendations are but a smattering that I offer to provide some suggestions for interesting reading.

THEOLOGY

Berry, R. J., ed. *The Care of Creation: Focusing Concern and Action*. Downers Grove, Ill.: InterVarsity Press, 2000.

Bradley, Ian. *God Is Green: Ecology for Christians*. New York: Image Books, 1992.

Fox, Matthew. *Original Blessing*. Sante Fe, N.M.: Bear & Company, 1983.

The Green Bible (NRSV). San Francisco: HarperOne, 2008.

McFague, Sallie. *The Body of God: An Ecological Theology*. Minneapolis: Fortress Press, 1993.

Nash, James A. *Loving Nature: Ecological Integrity and Christian Responsibility*. Nashville: Abingdon Press, 1991.

Northcott, Michael S. *A Moral Climate: The Ethics of Global Warming*. Maryknoll, N.Y.: Orbis Books, 2007.

Oelschlaeger, Max. *Caring for Creation: An Ecumenical Approach to the Environmental Crisis*. New Haven, Conn.: Yale University Press, 1994.

Robinson, Tri, and Jason Chatraw. *Saving God's Green Earth: Rediscovering the Church's Responsibility to Environmental Stewardship*. Norcross, Ga.: Ampelon Publishing, 2006.

Sleeth, J. Matthew. *Serve God, Save the Planet: A Christian Call to Action*. White River Junction, Vt.: Chelsea Green Publishing Co., 2006.

Van Dyke, Fred, David C. Mahan, Joseph K. Sheldon, and Raymond H. Brand. *Redeeming Creation: The Biblical Basis for Environmental Stewardship*. Downers Grove, Ill.: InterVarsity Press, 1996.

PSYCHOLOGY

Du Nann Winter, Deborah, and Susan M. Koger. *The Psychology of Environmental Problems*. 2nd ed. Mahwah, N.J.: Lawrence Erlbaum Associates, 2003.

Kasser, Tim. *The High Price of Materialism*. Cambridge, Mass.: MIT Press, 2002.

Kasser, Tim, and Allen D. Kanner, eds. *Psychology and Consumer Culture: The Struggle for a Good Life in a Materialistic World*. American Psychological Association, 2004.

McKenzie-Mohr, Doug, and William Smith. *Fostering Sustainable Behavior: An Introduction to Community-Based Social Marketing*. Gabriola Island, B.C.: New Society Publishers, 1999.

Roszak, Theodore. *The Voice of the Earth: An Exploration of Ecopsychology*. Grand Rapids, Mich.: Phanes Press, 2001.

Roszak, Theodore, Mary E. Gomes, and Allen D. Kanner. *Ecopsychology: Restoring the Earth, Healing the Mind*. San Francisco: Sierra Club Books, 1995.

Thomas, Susan Gregory. *Buy, Buy, Baby: How Consumer Culture Manipulates Parents and Harms Young Minds*. Boston: Houghton Mifflin, 2007.

ECOLOGY

Bach, David, and Hillary Rosner. *Go Green, Live Rich: 50 Simple Ways to Save the Earth (and Get Rich Trying)*. New York: Broadway, 2008.

Berry, Wendell, and Norman Wirzba, eds. *The Art of the Common-Place: The Agrarian Essays of Wendell Berry*. Washington, D.C.: Counterpoint Press, 2002.

Bongiorno, Lori. *Green, Greener, Greenest: A Practical Guide to Making Eco-Smart Choice a Part of Your Life*. New York: Perigee Books, 2008.

Carson, Rachel. *Silent Spring: 49th Anniversary Edition*. Boston: Houghton Mifflin, 2002.

Clark, Duncan, and Richie Unterberger. *The Rough Guide to Shopping with a Conscience*. New York: Rough Guides, 2007.

Gore, Al. *An Inconvenient Truth: The Planetary Emergency of Global Warming and What We Can Do About It*. New York: Rodale, 2006.

Imhoff, Daniel. *Paper or Plastic: Searching for Solutions to an Overpackaged World*. San Francisco: Sierra Club Books, 2005.

Kingsolver, Barbara, Steven L. Hopp and Camille Kingsolver. *Animal, Vegetable, Miracle: A Year of Food Life*. New York: HarperCollins, 2007.

Korten, David C. *The Great Turning: From Empire to Earth Community*. San Francisco: Berrett-Koehler Publishers, 2003.

Leopold, Aldo. *A Sand County Almanac*. New York: Oxford University Press, 1949/1968.

Louv, Richard. *Last Child in the Woods*. Chapel Hill, N.C.: Algonquin Books, 2005.

Macy, Joanna R., and Molly Young Brown. *Coming Back to Life: Practices to Reconnect Our Lives, Our World*. Stony Creek, Conn.: New Society Publishers, 1998.

McDonough, William, and Michael Braungart. *Cradle to Cradle: Remaking the Way We Make Things*. New York: North Point Press, 2002.

McKibben Bill. *Deep Economy: The Wealth of Communities and the Durable Future*. New York: Times Books, 2007.

Schildgen, Bob. *Hey, Mr. Green: Sierra Magazine's Answer Guy Tackles Your Toughest Green Living Questions*. San Francisco: Sierra Club/Counterpoint, 2008.

Schlosser, Eric. *Fast Food Nation: The Dark Side of the American Meal*. Boston: Houghton Mifflin, 2001.

Smith, Alisa, and J. B. MacKinnon. *Plenty: One Man, One Woman, and a Raucous Year of Eating Locally*. New York: Harmony Books, 2007.

Steffen, Alex, ed. *Worldchanging: A User's Guide for the 21st Century*. New York: Harry N. Abrams, 2008.

Suzuki, David, and Amanda McConnell. *The Sacred Balance: Rediscovering Our Place in Nature*. Amherst, N.Y.: Prometheus Books, 1997, 2007.

Van Der Ryn, Sim, and Stuart Cowan. *Ecological Design*. Washington, D.C.: Island Press, 1996, 2007.

Wilson, Edward O. *The Creation: An Appeal to Save Life on Earth*. New York: W. W. Norton, 2006.

References

ABC News. 2007. "Prayer to End Climate Change." Retrieved September 7, 2007, from *http://abcnews.go.com/print?id=3572327*.

American Dietetic Association. 2003. Press release dated June 3, 2003. Retrieved April 26, 2008, from *www.eatright.org*.

Anderson, E. E. 2007. *Eco-chic Weddings: Simple Tips to Plan an Environmentally Friendly, Socially Responsible, Affordable, and Stylish Celebration*. Long Island City, N.Y.: Hatherleigh.

Anderson-Stembridge, M., and P. D. Radford. n.d. National Council of Churches of Christ Eco-Justice Programs. "Bottom Line Ministries That Matter: Congregational Stewardship with Energy Efficiency and Clean Energy Technologies." Retrieved April 5, 2008, from *www.nccecojustice.org/network/downloads/BottomLine_5P.pdf*.

Asia-Pacific Economic Cooperation (APEC), Energy Standards Information System. 2008. "A Global Movement toward Phasing Out Energy Inefficient Light Bulbs Is Emerging." Retrieved May 5, 2008, from *www.apec-esis.org/whatsnew.php?id=100146*.

Association for Wedding Professionals International. 2008. Statistics for the wedding industry. Retrieved April 7, 2008, from *afwpi.com/wedstats.html*.

Axelrod, L. J., and P. Suedfeld. 1995. "Technology, Capitalism, and Christianity: Are They Really the Three Horsemen of the

Eco-Collapse?" *Journal of Environmental Psychology* 15: 183–95.

Barna Group. 2005. "Americans Give Billions to Charity, but Donations to Churches Have Declined." Retrieved April 18, 2008, from *www.barna.org.*

Brown, L. R. 1995. "Ecopsychology and the Environmental Revolution: An Environmental Foreword." In *Ecopsychology: Restoring the Earth, Healing the Mind,* ed. T. Roszak, M. E. Gomes, and A. D. Kanner, xiii–xvi. San Francisco: Sierra Club.

Catholic News Service. 2006. "Pope Warns against Environmental Damage, Says It Burdens World's Poor." Retrieved September 8, 2007, from *www.catholicnews .com/data/stories/cns/0604876.htm.*

Catholic News Service. 2007. "Patriarch, Pope Join in Plea for the Environment." Retrieved September 7, 2007, from *www.catholicnews.com.*

Christian Aid. 2008. "Time for Action on Climate Change." Retrieved June 5, 2008, from *www.christianaid.org.uk/images/ CAW08_cma_time_for_action.rtf.*

Cialdini, R. B. 2003. "Crafting Normative Messages to Protect the Environment." *Current Directions in Psychological Science* 12, no. 4: 105–9.

Clay, R. A. 2001a. "Green Is Good for You." *Monitor on Psychology* 32, no. 4. Retrieved September 2, 2007, from *www.apa.org/monitor/apr01/greengood.html.*

———. 2001b. "Many Approaches to Being Green." *Monitor on Psychology* 32, no. 4. Retrieved September 2, 2007, from *www.apa.org/monitor/apr01/greenapproach.html.*

Conn, S. A. 1995. "When the Earth Hurts, Who Responds?" In *Ecopsychology: Restoring the Earth, Healing the Mind,* ed. T. Roszak, M. E. Gomes, and A. D. Kanner, 156–71. San Francisco: Sierra Club.

DeWitt, C. B. 1994. *Earth-Wise: A Biblical Response to Environmental Issues.* Grand Rapids, Mich.: CRC Publications.

Earth Policy Institute. 2008. "Carbon Dioxide Emissions Accelerating Rapidly." Retrieved May 5, 2008, from *www.earth-policy.org/Indicators/CO₂/2008.htm.*

Ecumenical Patriarchate. 2005. Message for the volume of the 5th Halki seminar (April 18). Retrieved September 7, 2007, from *www.ec-patr.org.*

Environmental Protection Agency (EPA). 2008a. "Paper and Paperboard Products." Retrieved April 25, 2008, from *www.epa.gov/garbage/paper.htm.*

———. 2008b. "Plug-In to eCycling." Retrieved April 16, 2008, from *www.epa.gov/epaoswer/osw/conserve/plugin.*

Fair Trade Federation. 2008. Retrieved March 29, 2008, from *www.fairtradefederation.org.*

Frantz, C., F. S. Mayer, C. Norton, and M. Rock. 2005. "There Is No 'I' in Nature: The Influence of Self-Awareness on Connectedness to Nature." *Journal of Environmental Psychology* 25: 427–35.

Funeral Consumers Alliance. 2007. "Common Funeral Myths." Retrieved April 14, 2008, from *www.funerals.org.*

Glendale Memorial Nature Preserve. 2007. Retrieved April 14, 2008, from *www.glendalenaturepreserve.org.*

Gore, A. 2006. *An Inconvenient Truth: The Planetary Emergency of Global Warming and What We Can Do About It.* New York: Rodale.

Gravitz, A. 2006. "Matching the Scale of the Problem: Examining the Princeton CMI's Emissions Reduction Plan." *Co-op America Quarterly* (Fall): 13–15.

Green America. 2006. "Climate Solutions." *Co-op America Quarterly* 70 (Fall).

———. 2007. "Carbon Offsets Demystified." *Real Money* (March–April).

Greenpeace. 2008. *stopgreenwash.org.* Retrieved June 6, 2008.

Hiebert, T. 2000. "The Human Vocation: Origins and Transformations in Christian Traditions." In *Christianity and Ecology,* ed. D. T. Hessel and R. R. Ruether, 133–51. Cambridge, Mass.: Harvard University Press.

Imhoff, D. 2005. *Paper or Plastic: Searching for Solutions to an Overpackaged World.* San Francisco: Sierra Club Books.

Intergovernmental Panel on Climate Change (IPCC). 2007a. Retrieved September 9, 2007, from *www.ipcc.ch/about/index.htm.*

Intergovernmental Panel on Climate Change (IPCC). 2007b. "Summary for Policymakers." In *Climate Change 2007: Impacts, Adaptation and Vulnerability: Contribution of Working Group II to the Fourth Assessment Report of the Intergovernmental Panel on Climate Change,* ed. M. L. Parry, O. F. Canziani, J. P. Palutikof, P. J. van der Linden, and C. E. Hanson. Cambridge: Cambridge University Press. Retrieved September 4, 2007, from *www.ipcc-wg2.org/index.html.*

Intergovernmental Panel on Climate Change (IPCC). 2007c. "Summary for Policymakers." *Climate Change 2007: Synthesis Report.* Retrieved June 7, 2008, from *www.ipcc.ch/pdf/assessment-report/ar4/syr/ar4_syr_spm.pdf.*

Intergovernmental Panel on Climate Change (IPCC). 2007d. "Summary for Policymakers." In *Climate Change 2007: The Physical Science Basis: Contribution of Working Group I to the Fourth Assessment Report of the Intergovernmental Panel on Climate Change,* ed. S. Solomon, D. Quin, M. Manning, Z. Chen, M. Marquis, K. B. Averyt, M. Tignor, and H. L. Miller. Cambridge, UK, and New York: Cambridge University Press. Retrieved September 4, 2007, from *ipcc-wg1.ucar.edu/wg1/Report/AR4WG1_Print_SPM.pdf.*

Kaplan, S. 1995. "The Restorative Benefits of Nature: Toward an Integrative Framework." *Journal of Environmental Psychology* 15: 169–82.

Kasser, T. 2002. *The High Price of Materialism.* Cambridge, Mass.: MIT Press.

Kasser, T., R. M. Ryan, C. E. Couchman, and K. M. Sheldon. 2004. "Materialistic Values: Their Causes and Consequences." In *Psychology and Consumer Culture: The Struggle for a Good Life in a Materialistic World,* ed. T. Kasser and A. D. Kanner, 11–28. Washington, D.C.: American Psychological Association.

Mack, J. E. 1995. "The Politics of Species Arrogance." In *Ecopsychology: Restoring the Earth, Healing the Mind,* ed. T. Roszak, M. E. Gomes, and A. D. Kanner, 156–71. San Francisco: Sierra Club.

Marland, G., T. A. Boden, and R. J. Andres. 2007. "Carbon Dioxide Information Analysis Center (CDIAC), Oak Ridge National Laboratory, U.S. Global, Regional, and National CO_2 Emissions." In *Trends: A Compendium of Data on Global Change,* Department of Energy. Retrieved May 31, 2008, from *cdiac.ornl.gov/trends/emis/top2004.cap.*

McKenzie-Mohr, D., and W. Smith. 1999. *Fostering Sustainable Behavior: An Introduction to Community-Based Social Marketing.* Gabriola Island, B.C.: New Society Publishers.

Mertz, S. A., and A. Korfhage. n.d. "The Power of Fair Trade." In *Co-Op America: Guide to Fair Trade,* 4–7. (*Guide* available at *www.greenamericatoday.org/programs/fairtrade*).

MSNBC. 2007. "Pope Headlining Eco-Friendly Festival." Retrieved September 7, 2007, from *www.msnbc.msn.com/id/20535580/print/1.*

National Council of Churches of Christ Eco-Justice Programs. 2007. *www.nccecojustice.org.* Retrieved August 26, 2007.

Nierenberg, D. 2008. "Meat Output and Consumption Grow." Worldwatch Institute. Retrieved April 25, 2008, from *www.worldwatch.org/node/5443*.

Ouellette, P., R. Kaplan, and S. Kaplan. 2005. "The Monastery as a Restorative Environment." *Journal of Environmental Psychology* 25: 175–88.

Presbyterian Church USA. 2007. "Global Warming Likely to Increase Hunger: Hits the Poor Hardest." Retrieved September 4, 2007, from *www.pcusa.org/hunger/features/climate3*.

Presbyterian Hunger Program. 2007. Retrieved August 26, 2007, from *www.pcusa.org/hunger*.

Robinson, J. 2008. "What You Need to Know about the Beef You Eat." *Mother Earth News* 226 (February–March).

Robinson, T. 2006. *Saving God's Green Earth: Rediscovering the Church's Responsibility to Environmental Stewardship*. Norcross, Ga.: Ampelon Publishing.

Roszak, T. 1992, 2001. *The Voice of the Earth*. Grand Rapids, Mich.: Phanes Press.

———. Roszak, T. 1995. "Where Psyche Meets Gaia." In *Ecopsychology: Restoring the Earth, Healing the Mind*, ed. T. Roszak, M. E. Gomes, and A. D. Kanner, 1–17. San Francisco: Sierra Club.

Sierra. 2006. "My Low-Carbon Diet: From Gas Gluttony to Fuel Fitness in Three Weeks." *Sierra* (September/October): 50–57.

Sleeth, J. M. 2006. *Serve God, Save the Planet: A Christian Call to Action*. White River Junction, Vt.: Chelsea Green Publishing.

Spillman, P. 2008. "The ABCs of Unrelenting Waste." *E magazine* (March–April): 11–12.

Suzuki, D. 2007. *The Sacred Balance: Rediscovering Our Place in Nature*. Vancouver, B.C.: Greystone Books.

Tarver-Wahlquist, Sarah. 2007. "The Perils of E-Waste." *Co-op America Quarterly* 73: 28–31.

Tearfund. 2008. "The Bishop Speaks." Retrieved April 5, 2008, from *www.tearfund.org/Churches/Carbon+fast+new.*

TerraChoice Environmental Marketing Inc. 2007. "Six Sins of Greenwashing: A Study of Environmental Claims In North American Consumer Markets." Retrieved May 2, 2008, from *www.terrachoice.com.*

United Nations. 2006. "Livestock's Long Shadow: Environmental Issues and Options." *www.virtualcentre.org/en/library/key_pub/longshad/A0701E00.htm.* Retrieved April 25, 2008.

United Nations Framework Convention on Climate Change (UNFCCC). 2007a. *unfccc.int/kyoto_protocol/items/2830.php.* Retrieved May 12, 2008.

United Nations Framework Convention on Climate Change (UNFCCC). 2007b. Retrieved May 12, 2008, from *maindb.unfccc.int/public/country.pl?group=kyoto.*

United Nations Statistics Division, Common Database, Internet Users. 2008. Retrieved December 7, 2008, from *unstats.un.org/unsd/databases.*

U.S. Green Building Council. 2008. Resources, Green building research. Retrieved April 27, 2008, from *www.usgbc.org.*

World Council of Churches. 2007. "Minute on Global Warming and Climate Changes." Retrieved June 5, 2008, from *www.oikoumene.org/?id=5610.*

Index

(Terms in **bold face** can be found in resources, recommended readings, or reference sections.)